If you haven't read know Detective wonderful city of B

Here are some of the words written about the books of Steve Kenning:

'If you love Barcelona and you love reading fiction the chances are that you have spent a frustrating time searching for modern day fiction based in the city. Apart from Montalban, there is very little based in modern day Barcelona. Now though, there is a new Barcelona thriller writer on the scene, Steve Kenning.'

Barcelona Reporter

'A pacy thriller, that introduces readers to the delights of Barcelona.'

Evening Herald

'The book reflects very well the current atmosphere of Barcelona.'

Roma Bosch

Barcelona Betrayal
_____

Other books by Steve Kenning:

Thrillers:

La Hermandad del Noveno Noviembre
(The Brotherhood of the Ninth November)
– *introducing Detective Will Ferran*

Personal growth/self-help:

Positivity

The Art of Personal Mastery

A Handbook to Inspire

Acknowledgements

Having visited Barcelona for one day, more than twenty years ago, I decided to return a few years ago. The city had been transformed and presented a magical mix of culture, history, modernism and charm, without having lost the dark and sinister 'edge' of its recent past. It was a place I wanted to explore and discover.

I now enjoy living in the city for several weeks of the year and without the inspiration this wonderful place has given me I doubt I would ever have published even my first thriller.

In buying an apartment in the city, my wife and I came across a most charming and friendly solicitor, Roma Bosch. Roma not only helped us legally, he became a friend and now, along with his lovely wife, Cristina, they are introducing us gradually into the life and culture of the Catalan city.

Barcelona captures your imagination. I wanted to read about the city and, in particular, to read thrillers set in the city. I came across the writing of the great Manuel Vázquez Montalbán and his creation, the private detective Pepe Carvalho. Montalban's books generated ideas in my mind and helped, along with other writers, to shape my writing style. Finally, it takes a great amount of effort and time to write a book. I really enjoy the process but without the enthusiasm, support and enormous encouragement of my wife Paula I would not be a writer.

Steve Kenning

Barcelona Betrayal

To my wonderful mom

Steve Kenning.

Barcelona Betrayal

This novel is a work of fiction. The names, characters and incidents portrayed in it are the work of the author's imagination. Any resemblance to actual persons, living or dead, events or localities is entirely coincidental.

First published 2006

Copyright © Steve Kenning 2006

Pensadores Futuros

www.barca-only.com

British Library Cataloguing In Publication Data
A Record of this Publication is available from the British Library

ISBN 1846855012
978-1-84685-501-6

First Published 2006 by

Exposure Publishing, an imprint of Diggory Press, Three Rivers, Minions, Liskeard, Cornwall, PL14 5LE, UK
WWW.DIGGORYPRESS.COM

Steve Kenning

Barcelona Betrayal

Barcelona Betrayal

There's a man who spoke wonders,
Though I've never met him.
He said, 'He who seeks finds
And who knocks will be let in'
I think of you in motion
And just how close you are getting
And how every little thing anticipates you.
All down my veins my heart-strings call,
Are you the one that I've been waiting for?

Nick Cave

To Paula.
You are my only one.

Chapter 1

Enjoyment just wasn't the best word to describe her emotional state at that moment. Her mind was devoid of any sense of pleasure. The hall reverberated with ecstasy. It was so sultry, dripping with sweat and loud, almost as if she was standing inside the cavernous jowls of a huge, crazed killer whale hooked on listening to heavy rock. She was standing alone at the back of the hall. Half way up the seated terraces, right in front of the band. Her face was sullen. Her body was motionless. She looked like hell.

The overweight, young, hairy guy to her left kept looking at her, smiling at her. Each encouraging stare was carefully placed in between his yelps of delight and freeform dance movements that were at odds to the beat of the music. His sweat leapt from his body in all directions. He was having a great time, although he seemed to be thinking, 'How can 14,000 other people be enjoying themselves so much and you look so down?' He tried once again to get her involved. This time she again shrugged him off and then forced her way impolitely along the row of spectators, momentarily interrupting their dancing and enjoyment.

She just wasn't in the mood. It wasn't the location or the band. She just wanted something else. All

Barcelona Betrayal

that concerned her now was finding Jaume. He had disappeared to the toilet as soon as the Chilli Peppers had come on stage. That was over thirty minutes ago. This was meant to be fun. The last thing she wanted to do was to stand amongst a sweating crowd of music fans by herself, listening to a band she barely knew. It was Jaume who had bought the tickets and it was Jaume who had been so keen to see the Red Hot Chilli Peppers. He said he had seen them three times before and that he had all their CDs. That's what he said. Then he rushed off the moment they came on stage. Her idea of a good night was sitting in a bar drinking cava and then getting the balls together to sing karaoke songs. Something like Rod Stewart or Marty Pellow, certainly none of this crap.

She was fairly tall for a woman, 5 foot 6, but not particularly fit, and the steps out of the auditorium were steep and many. She was hot, agitated and tired. The noise from the band pummelled her eardrums. She raced up the steps to get to sanctuary. At last she hit the level walkway that skirted around the top floor entrance area to the Palau Sant Jordi. Here at least there were concrete walls that acted as a defence against the decibels. There was no one around. Everyone, even the security guards, was either inside the auditorium or as close to inside as possible. They were all keen to get as much as they could of the show. Maybe this band really were that good. Maybe she was

missing something. She shrugged to herself, 'I can't miss what I don't know I'm missing.'
This thought confused her but made her smile wryly to herself.

The exterior fire doors were open, probably to let some cool evening air into the sweltering arena. A blast of freshly cooled air hit her in the chest and took her by surprise. The flow enticed her to its source. Before long she was on the wide, concrete rimmed balcony that overlooked the rest of the Olympic Parc and onwards towards the El Prat airport. It was just dark. Lights splayed out across the cityscape. She leant on the concrete balcony. Immediately below her, some 200 metres away there were some teenagers playing what looked like baseball on a floodlit grass area. She couldn't be sure of what she was seeing in this light, although she had her lenses in which gave her eyesight a fighting chance. She skimmed the action below her. To the left she saw something glisten in the darkness. She moved towards it to get a better look. She found a vantage point right above what she presumed must be the delivery or service area to the Palau Sant Jordi. There were a few dim safety lights on the building and some reflected illumination from the floodlit ballpark, but very little other light. In the available light it was difficult to see anything clearly. She strained her eyes, trying to see through the semi-darkness.

There. There it was again. Something glistened. She stared intently. Fascinated. She could make out a shape, a body. The body was crouching behind a rubbish skip. The glistening was coming from something small. The shape held something in its hand. She stared and stared. It was a knife. On the third glisten she saw it clearly. The knife was no more than a small kitchen blade but it was held with intent. The figure moved very slightly, hardly at all. Listening. Listening for movements.

She glanced away from the crouching figure and focussed on a whistle. Coming out of the darkness alongside the building was another figure, a dark figure. Even in the summer heat at this late hour the approaching figure was wearing black and was covered all over. The whistling figure appeared not to have a care in the world. It was a man, or was it, she couldn't be sure, tall though, five foot eight, or so, in height. The figure strode purposefully towards the rubbish skips. She watched. Instinctively she knew what was coming next. She tried to scream, to call out, but nothing came out of her wide, open, gaping mouth. Fixated, she couldn't move. She watched.

Chapter 2

It was all over in seconds. The whistling figure lay in a crumpled heap on the invisible tarmac. It was hard to see the body, enveloped as it was in the dark shadows. The once crouching figure was now standing astride the dark shape that lay on the ground. There was a knife jutting upwards at a forty-five degree angle from the right hand of the assailant. She saw a dark liquid gradually run into a patch of floodlit tarmac. The body on the ground was motionless. In one quick movement the assailant hoisted up the limp carcass and tipped it into the rubbish skip. He closed the cover furtively and stepped into the light. As he brushed over his clothes he appeared to be looking for any traces of blood. His manner suggested he was happy with his condition and he quickly moved towards the Palau Sant Jordi entrance. The light from the ballpark caught the figure fully for a second. She was still staring intently at the incident. She stared at the face of the assailant as he passed through the light beam.

The shock sent her reeling backwards. She shuddered to a standstill and reached out for the parapet wall to steady herself, but it wasn't within her reach.

'Oh no!' she cried out as she fell heavily to the floor.

'Esta bien? Esta bien?' shouted a guard racing over to help her, as she lay prostrate and motionless on the ground. She scrambled to her feet with the help of the guard. She had no idea what he was saying to her or what was going on around her. All she could think about was what she had just seen. Her mind was replaying over and over again that last image. Exactly what had she seen? How could it be? Maybe she was mistaken? After several minutes of soul searching she was convinced she had actually seen her worst fears realised. She was sure it was Jaume. After a minute or so the guard was still with her, looking confused as he was getting no response to his questions and she seemed all over the place mentally. She slowly gathered herself together and, now that she was convinced of what she had seen, pulled the bemused guard to the edge of the parapet.

'Look! Look!' She pointed towards the area of the attack. The guard could see nothing as she pointed over towards the rubbish skips. He could speak no English and she could speak little Spanish. There was a stand-off period whilst they looked at each other, each asking the question, 'What is going on here?'

As she looked into the eyes of the guard it was obvious that there was little more to do or say here. It was clear that there was nothing to be seen at this distance and she couldn't find a way to ask how to get down to the skips. The guard looked at her with a very puzzled expression. She was obviously not hurt but she was in turmoil. What should he do? She could see the dilemma in his eyes. She took the initiative. After a few minutes she thanked the guard for his help and explained, with the help of gestures, that she had felt light headed but was now better. With that she headed back into the concert hall.

She was slowly stumbling down the steps to the auditorium when her right arm was grabbed above the elbow from behind. She was gently pulled around to face her lover, Jaume.
'Jaume!' she said in astonishment. She didn't know what else to say. He looked really good in the semi-darkness of the concert hall stairwell.
'I am so sorry. You must have been very worried. I needed to spend some time on the toilet and I could not find one with any toilet paper in. I have been all round this stadium. It must have been those chillies we ate last night.'
As he spoke he held his stomach.
'So you haven't been outside....down by the skips?'
'The skips? No. Why?' he replied incredulously.
'I just thought I saw you there,' she stuttered, confused in her thoughts. He certainly didn't look like he had just killed someone.
'I may have been forced out there if I had not found a toilet, but no, I have been very occupied,' he laughed.
'You look tired. Have you had enough of the band? It is late. Shall we go?'

'If you don't mind Jaume, I'm exhausted.'
With that Jaume held onto her arm and led her up and out of the arena. As they slowly walked across the wide-open courtyard at the front of the Palau Sant Jordi the music pulsated. The concert was nearing its climax and everyone was having a good time. She was not having a good time though. She was confused. Had she really seen what she thought she had seen? Was her lover a murderer? Her mind was distracted. She knew she must be wrong. Jaume was a loving and gentle man. He couldn't do such a thing. She was convinced that he wouldn't lie to her.

Chapter 3

They crossed the road looking for a taxi. Nothing around, just a few parents, sat motionless in their cars, waiting for their kids.

'Let's head down to the Plaça de España. There will be many taxis down there,' suggested Jaume.

She was in no state to disagree. She let him lead her across the road and into the park above MNAC, the wonderful art gallery that was housed in the palace that looked over the Fira exhibition park. The palace was high on a hill and you had to scale hundreds of steps or ride several escalators before you hit the Plaça de España.

'I love you so much Sandie,' smooched Jaume into the ear of the woman he held by the arm as they moved steadily down the parkland of the Palace. The escalator going down ahead of them was not working so they quickly stepped down the steps two at a time. They were in a hurry. The concert was nearly over and there would be a rush for the taxis down at the Plaça de España. Jaume held her by the arm, carefully and lovingly. She knew he loved her. She knew her vision of the stabbing was wrong. She had seen something and someone, but it definitely was not Jaume. She would wait until she was stronger, maybe in the morning, and then tell him, and maybe the police if he agreed, about what she had seen. Now was not the time. She was exhausted. Jaume was her strength. She rested her head on his shoulder as they skipped down the steps.

There were few people around. Darkness enveloped the whole area, although the walkways and escalators were well floodlit. Either side the darkness of the trees suffocated the infiltrating light. This was not a place to be alone. Within minutes though there would be thousands flooding down from the concert. She felt safe with Jaume. He was strong, positive and he knew how the world worked. They could see the Fira Plaza in front of them, another flight of stairs or an escalator and they were on the level heading to the taxi rank. The waterfall in front of the Palace thundered as they passed by. She was still in a daze. Her mind was wandering, without Jaume there what would she do? She felt light headed. She felt weak. Jaume was strong and he had her by the arm, leading her to a place she wanted to be. Somewhere away from the crowds, alone with Jaume, sharing a bottle of wine between them. He was guiding her to the taxis, to safety. She looked at Jaume. He was light haired, but not grey. He was in his late thirties but looked younger, he had some wrinkles but not many. He was her god. Her dream man, he was heaven-sent. What had she done to deserve him? Even in her present half-awake, unreal state she knew he was a dream. He loved her and she loved him. The vision she had had earlier was disappearing fast as they glided together, in unison, down the steps.

It happened so quickly that she didn't even realise. One moment she was heading down the escalator and across the pavement with Jaume and the next moment she was on the floor. She had no idea what happened. She lay on the cold, marble paving slabs in front of the Fira exhibition halls that stood at the base of the imposing MNAC Palace. Her head hurt at the back. She had a strange sensation there that made her think that blood might be trickling down the back of her head, although she felt disinclined to check it out. Where was Jaume? She could see a light high above her head. It was blurred and it yellowed as it merged into the dark background. The light started to rotate. She had no idea what she was looking at. Nothing was real. How long had she been lying there? It seemed like hours, although it was probably minutes. Suddenly, she was in the middle of a battlefield. Hordes of people flooded by her, running, shouting. Most ignored her, but a few stopped and stood over her. She looked up. Two faces, three faces, five faces. Faces she had never seen before. Their mouths were moving saying things she couldn't hear. Then it was as if her ears had suddenly popped, she heard their words.
'Are you OK?'
'What is wrong?'
'Can we help?'
'Who did this to you?'
Before long there were several people nursing her and others had called for the police.

Chapter 4

She wept. Her face looked ravaged by the tears that had created rivulets across her cheeks over the past hour. She wept more. The weeping turned into a deep, sorrowful sobbing. She was revealing her inner soul. She was a women bereft of anything. She had no self-worth, no one to care for her and she seemed to value nothing. There was another woman in the room with her. The woman said nothing. The woman stood some ten metres away, resting with her hands behind her back, nonchalantly watching her. The woman had been sympathetic at first and tried to console her. Yet after an hour or more of this bleating she had decided that the only way forward was to take on the suicide watch. You could see it in her eyes. The woman thought she was either a complete drama queen or on the verge of a breakdown. Female police officers have little heart.

She sat on a grey, moulded plastic chair. The black metal legs dug into the linoleum floor that was pitted black from the violence of the furniture and from the years of discarded cigarette butts. She was leant forward on her arms. Her elbows rested in the centre of the white, melanine-topped table. There was nothing else in the interview room. The white table had galvanised metal legs and was strong and rigid. The table was in the centre of the room. She rested her pink-faced head in her hands.

The table surface was flooded with her tears. The liquid had spread and, due to the unevenness of the table, was dripping slowly onto the floor. She wore little. Her halter neck top was lurid green and her ample breasts pushed the material to its limits. Her size and shape were in control but there were the tell tale signs of increasing age and a lack of exercise around her stomach and thighs. As she leant forward onto her elbows her legs were dragged back under her chair and the cellulite was clear, high on her thigh, just below her raised, short, white, denim skirt. Her outfit was completed by her white, leather sandals, which both lay undisturbed, away from her feet, beneath the table.

The policewoman had a clear air of confusion on her face. She had been present for the whole time, hearing the statement and then the interview. The past hour had been spent listening to her sob. An attractive woman, in her early thirties and in pretty good shape, she was used to this duty. Hours spent with a witness or a suspect. It gave her thinking time and she liked to play games in her mind. It kept her sane. Her favourite game was to imagine the life of the other person in the room. With all the tears it was hard to tell anything about this one, although she looked attractive if not pretty. Her taste in clothes was expensive, but she was certainly not classy. The woman wondered what she did for a job, she wondered why she had not met an Englishman and settled down in London.

The woman had always dreamed of doing that herself one day. That thought took her off to somewhere different.

Chapter 5

The only things that disturbed the perfect symmetry of the interview room were the door and a one-way window. The door suddenly began to open inwards, the white painted, heavy, wooden door moved into the room very slowly. Almost apologetically, a man crept into the room around the half opened door. As soon as the whole of his body was in the room he carefully and quietly closed it. He stood in silence, looking first at the policewoman standing at the back of the room. She nodded a welcome to him, then his eyes focussed on the sobbing heap sat at the table. He observed for a few minutes, not saying anything and trying to make no sound. It was clear that the visitor was finding it very difficult to be discreet as he was at least six foot five inches tall and had a real presence. He was successful though, she hadn't noticed him.
'Senorita Shaw?'
'Senorita Shaw? Are you feeling any better?'
This, he immediately realised, was a stupid question as the mere words led to a renewed onslaught of wailing and sobbing.

The visitor moved towards the other chair in the room. It was placed directly opposite the table. He lifted it with one hand and turned it around. He wanted to be in control of this situation. He wanted to have a superior position, but standing would be too removed from her. He also didn't want to get anywhere near the liquid mess on the table. He sat on the chair and leaned his arms on the backrest. His huge frame dwarfed the chair. He was within two feet of the table. There was still no response from her.

He sat quietly looking at her for quite sometime. He glanced at the woman at the back of the room as if looking for permission. Then his manner changed. He had decided that after the two hours or so that this woman had spent in the interview room, taking up valuable police time, there was no excuse for this kind of behaviour. He had come into the room very sympathetic towards her and on her terms but she hadn't even registered him yet. Sympathy and empathy were two things that were in short supply in his make-up. He wasn't used to hanging around for answers either.
'Senorita Shaw.' His voice was slightly raised and agitated.
'You are sitting in the interview room of the Mossos d'Esquadra on Gran Via Corts Catalanes at 6.05 a.m on the 15th July. I am Detective Ferran and I am here to interview you further following our initial investigations in respect of the report you made to my colleague at 3.30 am this morning.'
She barely moved. Her head was still hidden in her hands on the table. She stopped her loud sobbing just enough to hear what he had said.

He looked at her incredulously.

'Senorita Shaw!' His voice was significantly louder. 'You are not a suspect in a crime. You, in fact, have reported a crime and are looking for our support. Why then will you not speak to me?'

The policewoman was taken aback by the pitch of his voice and stood to attention almost involuntarily. Her gaze looked across to the table willing some form of response. She lifted her head and slowly looked at Ferran. Her face was a mess. Make-up ran riot around all parts of her eyes and cheeks, both of which were red raw. Her hair was matted and sodden. Ferran looked carefully at her and then glanced away. She was not a pretty sight. She still said nothing.

'If you do not speak to me I will have you arrested for wasting police time. I have been called on duty to take on this case two hours earlier than I am due. I do not intend this to be a waste of my time.'

'I'm so sorry...I'm so sorry. I just want Jaume back,' she wailed again.

Ferran was having none of his. He had seen distress a hundred times and he had seen many women cry, but not like this. He hated weakness and inefficiency of any sort. He felt he was looking at a weak, pathetic woman. He ordered the policewoman at the back of the room to get some tissues and a coffee. She quickly hurried out of the room to fetch them.

Chapter 6

Detective Will Ferran was every woman's dream of a near middle-aged man. He knew it, but he didn't know it. He knew he was attractive to woman but he could never really quite believe that he was, resulting in a complete lack of arrogance. Men envied him as he had an almost animal attraction to women but he was seemingly so cool he didn't ever take advantage of it. Most men make their attraction and intention towards women very evident. To most men anything in a short skirt, with reasonable sized breasts, is attractive and ripe for the taking, the hunt on. A few lewd comments here and there to impress their mates and they would be away, heading for a good fuck. If she didn't want to know then she was probably some kind of tease or prude. Ferran wasn't like most men. He knew he was OK to look at and he knew he was good at his job. He emanated an aura of confidence. However, this never led him to take any kind of liberty with any woman. He had a certain taste in women and he was very particular. Some women repulsed him. They were too open and easy with men. Despite this view he respected all women, he would never abuse a woman. He was a protector and a gentleman. He hated the male, chauvinistic, bullying, maltreatment of women. This made him even more attractive to most women. It wasn't just his aura and his attitude towards women that was a turn on for them. He was six foot five, very tall for a Spaniard, probably a result of his English mother's gene pool, and dark-haired, with not a hint of grey. He was slim, had good personal habits and dressed well, if sometimes a little scruffily. In his mind's eye he saw himself as a Bryan Ferry look-a-like, the lead singer of the seventies rock group Roxy Music. Ferran was an enigma, and enigmas are not always popular.

Chapter 7

Ferran pushed back his lank hair from his forehead with his right hand in exasperation. His hair was long for a man of his age. Different. He was style conscious, it was not too long. He liked it that way. He leant forward and engaged the woman eye to eye for the first time. She looked back. This time she could see and feel his strength. This guy was not to be messed with. He could visibly feel her engage and register an interest in what he was saying. He gradually felt the vibe he felt with most women as they began to explore him verbally and visually. He usually accepted it as normal female procedure, but this time he knew she was looking for a weakness, for a way to get ahead in their conversation. He was having none of it, she was a weak woman, and he knew it.

'Your statement earlier outlined a number of very serious incidents and you were very graphic in all your descriptions.'

He paused deliberately and looked at her demeanour. She had stopped sobbing and was trying to regain some semblance of dignity. She was fiddling with her hair and wiping her eyes. The woman police officer came back in at that moment with tissues and a plastic cup of coffee that she placed down on the table in front of her without a word. The woman police officer then resumed her place against the wall. The tissues were used up immediately. Half of them just soaked up the tears that had flooded the table. The others she used to wipe her face. The coffee looked cold but she threw it down her throat. Ferran continued to stare at her. He could feel her discomfort as his eyes began to probe deep inside her. She looked a complete mess. She was no match for him. He wanted the truth. He felt from the first moment that she wasn't an honest woman. He had the facts in his hand.

'This first statement you made, several hours ago, is inaccurate.'

He held a paper file up in his left hand as he spoke. She just stared back at him expressionless.

'There was no body in the skip at the Palau Sant Jordi when our officers went back there tonight. There was no blood on the ground where you described it. The guards at the Palau Sant Jordi have all been interviewed and none of them remember seeing or speaking to you. There is also no record anywhere, in España or England, of a Jaume Magi Medina, your alleged lover.'

He delivered these words slowly, with sternness, whilst watching her every emotion.

'You cannot be serious... Mr.. er... Detective... Fe.... rran.' She gasped.

'How do you expect me to take you seriously when you talk nothing but crap,' he pounced. She looked up at him. Her head was separated from her arms that were still resting on the sodden table.

'I saw what I saw....Why would I tell a lie?' She looked amazed at him.

'And I have lived with and loved Jaume for the past year. What do you mean there is no record? Are you saying he doesn't exist?'

Ferran loved this. He knew she was acting. She wasn't that good. What was she playing at though? He needed to find out what her game was.

'Senorita Shaw, I am not saying that we do not believe you, but we could find no evidence of the killing, the abduction, or even of your boyfriend. Are you sure about the facts?'

Ferran stared at her. He met her green eyes. They flinched as he spoke. Then they hardened their stare. She met him head on, but he knew. He knew she was lying.

She was struggling. This detective really fancied himself. He spoke with such conviction. She didn't expect this. He was obviously top quality. She was a bad actor and she knew it. He knew it. She had thought her tears and histrionics would pull anyone onto her side. But no, this guy was unreal. He was hard. He didn't do emotion. She felt he could see through her. What should she do? She had nobody to speak to. She paused for a few minutes. She could sense the agitation of the detective. She still said nothing. She needed time to think, a new angle, another approach. Why was he looking at her like that? He unnerved her. She found him attractive but she hated him. Why didn't he just go along with her story? Surely that was the easiest way.

Ferran was searching inside her with his eyes. What was this time-waster all about? Why had he, the most effective and successful detective on the Mossos, been given this case? It was so obvious that this woman wanted attention, a sad and lonely person. For all he knew she had made up the whole situation and the story about having a boyfriend. Whatever, he wanted to finish the whole thing now. If only he could get her to admit it was all a waste of time, it was all make-believe.

She gulped the rest of the cold coffee down. The cup, plastic and empty, was placed back on the table. She tried to salvage her position.
'I accept, Detective Ferran, that I may not have seen what I thought I had seen concerning the murder. I couldn't believe it myself.' She gulped again.
'But.' As she spoke she sat back for the first time.
'But, I do know that Jaume exists and I was with him when he was taken from me....and I need you to find him.' She splurted this out before she again burst into tears.

Ferran said nothing. He looked at the women police officer that was standing motionless at the back of the room. His expression was saying, 'What do you think?'
Her silent reply was, 'I don't believe a word she is saying.'
Ferran needed to move things on.

'OK. You are free to go. We will continue to look for your friend. Go back to your apartment. We will be in touch.'

He stood up and strode towards the door purposefully. He opened the door and spoke again before he left the room.

'We know there is much more to this case. We will discover it. Please do not leave the city.'

She stared back at him as she leant against the back of her chair. Whilst she was instantly relieved that the ordeal was over, she could relax now, she was distraught. She hadn't convinced the police.

Chapter 8

Ferran slammed the door as he left the interview room. The shudder reverberated along the corridor. It was early morning and there were few other sounds. He didn't lose his cool often, but the Englishwoman had really annoyed him. She was weak, he just knew she was, he could tell. In his eyes she was pathetic, yet she was sticking to her story. Why? What was her game? He knew she had an angle and she refused to move from it. He had been in this business for too long not to realise when someone was playing games. He strode down the whitewashed, illuminated corridor that ran from the interview room to the main area of detective office bases. Why was he so angry? His head rushed with blood and thoughts. He was consumed with the belief that his anger this morning was due to him being given this particular case. It was an easy one. Why give it to him? Give it to the trainee detectives straight out of university. They could spend hours on it. They could cut their teeth on it. He, Detective Ferran, had been there, had done it. Surely in this wonderful city, there were more substantial, meaty, cases he could work on. He was good. They all knew it. His mind fought with these thoughts. He was already in a bad mood and he could feel it building into an even worse mood. Why, he didn't know. He often liked these simple cases as they stimulated him and helped him keep in touch with reality. Today though, he didn't want the bother. Maybe it was his age. He was nearing forty-five. Recently he had started questioning what his life was about. He liked his work. He liked being good at it. He had devoted his life to it. He had no kids, a failed marriage, no real friends, a very small family by Spanish standards, just a sister and a mother. Increasingly he wanted more from his life. He loved to write, he could be the next Montalban, or so he thought in his dreams. He did well with women but none of them lasted. He couldn't forge a lasting relationship with anyone, let alone a woman, apart from Maria perhaps. Or at least he hoped. He dwelled on this thought for a moment as he stepped into the huge room that was home of all the detectives on the Gran Via. The room was on the first floor of a very grand apartment block in the Eixample Derecha, the part of the city that was planned out in grids during the early part of the twentieth century. The apartment building was quite wonderful, grandiose and foreboding, but at the same time welcoming and accessible. The room he walked into had been several apartments now knocked into one huge office. The ceiling was high and there was a spacious feel to it. The white walls helped. Each of the detectives worked in their own small, partitioned area. As he strode down the central aisle he was not feeling good vibes. He scowled at anyone who said hello. Why was he behaving like this? He was asking himself this question most of the time at the moment. He wasn't happy. He had felt recently that there was more to life. He didn't know why but he was very dissatisfied. His mood had gone too far. He wasn't even trying to reason with himself. He was looking for something to help release his venom.

Chapter 9

'Cracked her Ferran?' Roared Desanyo. Ferran hadn't seen him. He was surprised by his voice. Small, fat and annoying, with a brain similar in size and nature to that of a rodent, was how Ferran viewed the Detective. Desanyo was leaning back in his chair smiling. He could tell by Ferran's body language that he hadn't got anything from the woman. Another detective was sitting opposite him, mirroring Desanyo's actions. Ferran glanced at Martes. He really, really disliked this jumped-up excuse for a detective. Smarmy and unattractive, personality had totally bypassed this creature. He looked at his mouth. Martes was licking his lips. He had this habit of quickly licking his lips several times just before he made a wisecrack at someone else's expense. True to form, Martes joined in with the baiting.

'She's English isn't she? I would have thought with your blood you would have fucked her by now.' He jeered.

Ferran flipped. He hated the majority of the other male detectives at Gran Via. The young ones were OK, but the older ones were chauvinists, bigots and parochial. They were also pretty thick and corrupt, according to the book of Ferran. He felt nothing but pure rage as he flew through the air towards Martes. It all happened so quickly. Perhaps it was because of the early hour, Ferran didn't normally wake fully until 10 a.m, and today it was not yet 7

a.m. Had he had time to take in what he was doing, he would have loved the shocked expression on the face of his fellow detective. Martes was nailed to his chair as he watched the six foot five inches of Ferran flying towards him through the air. The right foot of Ferran was stretched out in front of him as, almost in slow motion, his right heel smashed into the nose of Detective Martes. The impact was instant. Martes fell to the floor. The blood splattered everywhere. The flow and spray was immediate. As Ferran landed in a clump on the ground amidst a mess of office stationery, Martes was struggling to his feet, holding his broken nose trying to stem the flow of blood and the pain.
'You bastard, you have broken my nose. You bastard.' He ran away from the scene, trailing blood over all the paperwork and making a lot of noise. Desanyo looked on, stunned. He couldn't believe it. His body language showed that he wasn't going to take on this madman though. He sat still, looking at Ferran.

Ferran was totally shocked by his actions. He had wanted to douse Martes for some time, although this just was not his style. This kind of behaviour brought him down to their level. What had happened? Why had he flipped and acted in that way? He couldn't come to terms with his actions. He was breathing heavily. The adrenalin was pumping through his body. He stood up gingerly. He was getting too old to be flying around offices.

His expensive black suit was crumpled, even more than usual. He dusted himself down and moved away from the scene of the crime. As he did so a number of people rushed over to the incident. Ferran moved towards his desk calmly and sat down heavily into the cushioned revolving chair. He sank deeply into the soft chair, staring at his computer screen with his head below the partition screens that separated him from the gathering crowd. He switched on his PC and looked blankly at it. There was nothing to look at but it gave him a few moments to gather his thoughts. The crowd hummed and discussed the action, but there was nothing to see, it had all happened so quickly. Within a few minutes everyone had returned to their posts. Ferran raised his head above the partitions that separated the detectives and surveyed the room. There was no sign of Martes or Desanyo. He placed his arms on the keyboard in front of him and rested his head on them. He knew he had taken things just that little bit too far.

Chapter 10

It wasn't long before the Jefe Perez Camps came within range of Ferran's field of vision. He took his time. Ferran had been looking up towards the far end of the huge room and caught sight of the chief moving towards him. Ferran liked Perez Camps, Jorge Perez Camps. He was new to the city and wasn't sullied by long-standing relationships and loyalties. He was also very professional. Jefe Perez Camps was a six-foot tall bull of a man. In his fifties but black haired without a hint of grey. He always looked as if he needed to shave, although he was always immaculately shaven and dressed. Ferran noticed his pink shirt with perfectly complementary blue tie. Ferran also noticed his demeanour, he wasn't happy.

Jefe Perez Camps approached Ferran and pulled up a comfy office chair to speak to him. He was professional. He wasn't going to shout, but you could tell he wanted to. This man was annoyed. But so was Ferran, although the pleasure of smashing his foot into Martes' face had acted like a release valve and he was gradually coming down from the heights of his anger. Jefe Perez Camps could see the condition Ferran was in. He didn't like dealing with this kind of situation, but he never shirked a challenge and it had to be done. He was a skilled tactician.
'I like you Ferran,' he started.

'You are a policeman after my own soul. You are true and honest.'

As he spoke Ferran knew that this was just the softener.

'But,' and he paused.

'You don't seem to like other people.....no, let me rephrase that.......you are very good with most people, but you do not seem to like your fellow detectives.' His look was like that of a teacher chastising a pupil, although the chastising hadn't started yet.

Ferran knew the game Perez Camps was playing, he had played it himself so many times before. Reason with the person, build them up a little then bring out the bad news. He stared hard into the inspector's eyes, willing him to cut the crap and to get on with what he had to say.

'If I am a man after your soul, then you will understand why I behaved as I did, Jefe,' returned Ferran.

'I really did not intend harm to Martes, although he fully deserved it,' he continued.

Perez Camps looked at him thoughtfully. It was obvious that he had a decision to make. Ferran knew that his Chief supported his views but that in his position he had to take action because of what he had done. There had to be some sense of order and a common code of conduct in the police.

'I think I know why you attacked Detective Martes but I cannot condone it. There are ways of handling such situations that do not involve violence.' As he spoke he moved his eyes from Ferran's to the floor and then back again.

'However, you are one of our best detectives Ferran. But..........I just don't believe that there are many of the other detectives that you can work with. Apart, of course, from Maria. You.....this.... gives me a real problem. Whilst I think of a solution I have no alternative than to suspend you from duty, unofficially.' He wasn't smiling, but his eyes had a hint of dismay and, strangely, support in them. Ferran didn't understand this. He wasn't surprised by the suspension, but by the attitude of the chief.

Chapter 11

'Unofficially,' the Jefe whispered.
'Because……' He looked furtively around him. He did not want anyone to hear him.
'I need you to keep working. Look into this case with the English woman. I think this is much bigger than is initially obvious. I will think of a solution to your, and now my, problem. I will be in touch. Now go!'
Ferran stared at his Jefe as he spoke. The sweat was pouring off his senior. Ferran looked into his eyes. They were honest and supportive, but he was doing what he had to do. Ferran realised he had gone too far. One side of his brain felt really good, as he knew Martes had been asking for it for a long time, but on the other side of his brain he was really annoyed with himself for his loss of control, and possibly loss of his job. He loved being an investigative detective. He knew he was good. He sat slumped in his black office chair. He pushed against his desk and the chair rolled backwards. At the same time he held Jefe Perez Camps in his vision. He liked the man, but he had to react to what he was saying for the sake of both his own reputation and that of the Jefe. Everyone had to think that the Jefe had dealt with him severely.
'You are as bad as those other pig-fuckers,' Ferran shouted as he stood up indignantly. He surprised himself with his own language. He tried to moderate it.

'I am sorry to abuse you Jefe, but I do not regret what I did to Martes. He was born without a mother!' With that statement Ferran launched his large frame down along the main walkway of the long room. He chose the longest route and strode purposefully to make the most impact. The huge room was silent as he took several minutes to reach the double doors at the end. Everyone else in the room was in suspended animation. Conversations had stopped, all eyes were looking his way and it even seemed as if the telephones had stopped ringing for a few seconds. Ferran looked straight ahead as he ate up the floor with his large feet. He was enjoying this performance. He held his head high as he walked through the doors. Outside, in the hallway, he stopped. He waited for the double doors to close behind him and then breathed out a huge sigh of relief. He paused for a moment and then took the lift to the ground floor. There he loitered for a few minutes. It wasn't long before Jefe Perez Camps joined him. The chief saw him immediately, walked quickly over to him, took hold of Ferran's arm at the elbow and forcibly guided him out through the main entrance of the building on to the Gran Via. They walked along the road, heading north.

Ferran was surprised by the strength of the Jefe. He didn't resist. His interest was growing.
'Ferran. I want to tell you something very important. It is something that only a few of my

superiors know. I am telling you because at this moment in time you need me as an ally and, in the future, I will certainly need your help.' Jefe Perez Camps had moved his right arm up around the shoulder of Ferran. This must have been strange to look at from behind as Ferran was several inches the taller of the two men. Ferran was again surprised by these words. The Chief was continually keeping him guessing with his actions and words. He stopped and faced his superior officer. Perez Camps was calm and relaxed. He had an inner strength that appeared to form the frame to his body. His skin seemed to lie on top of a rigid steel shell. He looked deep into Ferrans eyes. He didn't blink.

'You do not know this,' continued the Jefe in a serious, dramatic tone.

'But I have been brought into this force to clean up the likes of Martes and Desanyo.'

Ferran smiled to himself inwardly. He had guessed that there was much more to the Jefe.

'There is a good deal of inefficiency, poor practice and possibly corruption in this force at detective level,' continued Perez Camps.

'My role is to make the Mossos the best force in Europe. You know there is a problem, you have known for a long time. That is why you feel the way you do, but your actions today are not the way to deal with it. You have acted too quickly and too strongly.'

Ferran was surprised but heartened by these words. He looked at the Jefe.

'I cannot have someone like you around whilst I take these people on. You are too much of a distraction and you make them nervous. I need you out of the way. My problem though is that I need you to keep working. I will be in touch tomorrow. Go home now.'

Ferran didn't really know what to think. His mind was in a complete whirl. He found himself shaking hands with Perez Camps, this strong man, and looking at him with admiration. Then he turned and walked off by himself. He didn't look back.

Chapter 12

She sat at the table for some time. The crying had stopped. The questions had stopped. She was thinking. She was trying to put together a clearer picture of what had happened the previous evening. She hadn't slept now for nearly 24 hours. The clock, white plastic rim, red numbers and black hands, hung silently high on the wall of the interview room. It was 8.45 a.m. She caught a glimpse of the woman police officer at the back of the room as she glanced up at the clock. She hadn't noticed her before. She had been so consumed with her own grief and with the role she was trying to play. The officer was livid with boredom. She could see that the woman had been told to be there, to watch over her, but she must have been there for several hours. The female officer glowered back at her.

'I'm going now,' she said gingerly as she got up to leave the room. The officer jumped at the opportunity and shot over to her to help her out of the white room.

As she left the room she asked for the toilet. The woman officer stayed with her and showed her the way. The police officer was a real professional, you could see her mind working, 'Six hours or more with this woman and there is no way I am going to let her out of my sight until she is well gone.'

The two women walked slowly into the toilet. It was surprisingly clean and modern for a police station. New mirrors, flowers on a vanity unit, white walls and no graffiti. The flowers gave their perfume to the room. She went into a cubicle. After a few minutes the officer rapped on the door and asked if she was OK. She came out of the cubicle where she had been sitting, thinking. Thinking about what had happened. It was a blur, 'What had happened?'

She walked over to the plastic surrounded mirror. White plastic, shaped like an oval. She stared at the image in front of her. Her face was better. The redness had long gone and her eyes had recovered. Her make-up was staining the sides of her face. She washed herself quickly. She took another look in the mirror. Better. Much better. Her hair though, she couldn't go out in public with her hair looking like it did. It was matted and tangled. Her handbag was still with her. She hadn't noticed before, but it had never left her side. It was automatically there. No question. She unzipped the black leather edged zip. It was an expensive bag, or so it looked. Prada, at least a Prada copy, Jaume had given it to her. He had said it was from some expensive shop along the Passeig de Gracia. She had instantly thought it was from one of the African hawkers around the Port Vell. She didn't care. It was a gift from her lover, her man. She found a comb inside and

repaired her hair. Within minutes she had applied make-up and made herself feel like a woman again.
'Right,' she exclaimed.
'Now I am ready to leave this place.'
As she walked out of the toilet she instinctively touched the back of her head. It was sore. She touched her head then looked at her fingers. No blood. 'OK then let's move on,' she thought to herself. The toilet was near to the main entrance of the Mossos D'Esquadra building and she quickly crossed the entrance foyer and stepped out into the street. Outside she stopped and looked back through the glass doors. The female police officer visibly relaxed and let out a sigh of relief. She turned and marched defiantly down Gran Via. She was feeling much better.

Chapter 13

The feeling lasted probably a hundred yards. She didn't know where she was or where she was going. Her energy levels were exhausted. There was a café over the road. It took her a few minutes to negotiate the crossing on this very busy road, then, she stumbled into the café and onto a stool at the café bar.
'Café cortado y croissant chocolate, por favor,' she instructed.
The barman looked at her with caution in his eyes as he turned his back to her to work the coffee machine. He glanced over his shoulder as he did so. He was probably near the end of his shift and didn't want the hassle of a deranged woman in his bar. Within a couple of minutes he placed the cortado and the croissant in front of her, uttered a few words and scuttled off to the far end of the bar to serve his regulars.

She didn't acknowledge the barman or look at what he had served her. She had done a reasonably good job at making herself look presentable. Her make-up looked fine, she was a skilled practitioner in that area, and her face had lost the redness from all the crying, but she looked dog-tired, like she hadn't slept for a week. The bags beneath her eyes could hold a week's shopping. She slumped over her coffee, the steam from it drifting upwards, hitting her chin before dispersing. She stared at nowhere.

Barcelona Betrayal

All she could think of was Jaume. What had she really seen last night? Was it really him? Where was he now? Why hadn't he been there to look after her when she was knocked to the ground? She couldn't understand any of it. Yesterday morning life was the best it had ever been for her. Today it was the worst. Yesterday, she was in love with a man who really loved her. She was living in a wonderful city and they had had great sex before sipping coffee on the balcony of their small apartment overlooking the new Barceloneta market. The sun had been shining into their bedroom as they awoke and the careless feeling that had grasped them at that moment had been memorable. That was yesterday though, that wonderful feeling of carelessness and contentment. She put her hand forward, and without even looking at the small glass, her fingers found the cortado and lifted it to her lips. It tasted good. Her brain was put into half-gear. It was telling her that she needed energy, that she needed food. Her hand put the glass of coffee down on the counter. Her eyes searched the foot or so of the counter in front of her and located the croissant. Instinctively, with two hands she picked it up and devoured it. It was gone in seconds. She knew what she wanted, what she needed.

'Señor, otro cortado y croissant,' she shouted. The barman leapt to attention and busied himself with the order. It was soon sitting right in front of her.

The food hit her stomach and acted like an adrenalin shot. She could feel her energy levels rising. She could think with a little more clarity. She drifted back in her mind some ten years in time. She could see herself clearly. She was in her early twenties. Life was fun. She worked hard and played hard. Work fuelled her social life. Two weeks in Ibiza each year, with every Friday and Saturday in the clubs around Maidenhead where she lived. She worked in a finance office. She made good money for her age. Bleached blonde, nice clothes, fast car. She was a turn-on. She had three really good girlfriends. They went everywhere together. They did everything together. She shuddered slightly as she remembered a night in Ibiza when they picked up four guys and each had sex with them, a real orgy, or at least that is what her mind told her, in reality she had been so out of it on all kinds of spirits that she had no recollection of anything other than what her friends had told her late into the afternoon of the next day. At first she had been a real catch. She remembered even turning guys down, really attractive guys, waiting for the ones she wanted. But she had had a rule in those days, don't go with him if you don't want to shag him, and there were few she didn't go with. Ibiza was good because there were always new men. She paid the price once or twice though. After a couple of years of this routine, Maidenhead got boring. It was the same guys again and again and there were even some guys who didn't want it

Barcelona Betrayal

again. She frowned. She remembered the day, or the night to be exact, when it all fell apart. She was with one of her mates, the other two were married by then, in a nightclub in Reading. It was a normal Friday night. They were on the look-out for one or two guys they fancied and hadn't had. She was twenty-nine. An older, good-looking guy was hitting on her. He was nice and he was in good condition, but he was at least in his forties. He wouldn't leave her alone. He said she was 'ideal for him.' In the end she slapped him. He called her a slag. She stopped thinking about the past for a second. She sipped her cortado. That was it, she remembered. That was the moment she had decided to change her life. She should be proud of herself, she told herself in her head. If she hadn't done something about her life she would still be clubbing as a sad old slag now, probably like her friend Claire. That comment had stirred her. She had stormed out of the club, got in a taxi and cried in front of the mirror at home. She had looked deeply into the mirror and asked herself what she saw. She had replied that she was a tart, an easy lay, a conquest for a young lad, but she had no future. She had seen it all of a sudden and accepted it. She placed the cortado on the counter. She glanced at the barman who was keeping an eye on her. He knew she needed refuelling. As he made another, she fed herself the second croissant. Her energy levels growing as she did so. She wasn't moving anywhere but her mind was racing.

Chapter 14

Her thoughts moved forward to a couple of years ago. She had stopped clubbing, moved to central London and taken up a respectable job with a merchant bank. She had immediately felt much better about herself, but she was very lonely. She had few friends in this new world she had created and she was unsure as to how to make them. She tried speed-dating – no good, she just met some real weirdos. She tried internet ads and newspaper ads, these too only brought more heartache until the very last reply she'd had to an advert placed in the London Evening Standard. The reply was from a lonely thirty-something Spaniard, stranded in a strange city, on a remote island, a long way from his home and needing some cherishing. She had known instantly that this was the one. Jaume and her had met, fallen in love, moved to Barcelona when his training had ended in London and set up home together. They were so much in love that they had a joint mortgage on their apartment, a joint bank account and life insurance. That had been six months ago. She shuddered. Suddenly she remembered where she was and why she was here. The barman placed her third cortado in front of her. He tried a friendly smile, but she was still in her own world. He retreated to the regulars once again.

She left the steaming cortado and staggered off towards the toilets. They weren't hard to find even in her distracted state. She ploughed through the door and sat on the seat. It was dark and she struggled, with her hand smashing against the wall, to find a light switch. Her fingers connected with a small plastic button and there was light. She peed and thought. Nothing.

She sat there for several minutes not thinking, her head in her hands and her elbows resting on her knees. Then she saw a cracked tile just to her right. The tiles were white and well presented but there was just one with a crack in it. It had obviously cracked when they had laid the tiles, as there was tile cement in between the crack. This concerned her. What kind of craftsman could do such a job? And why wasn't it checked and put right? She was still troubling with this thought whilst she stood up, pulled up her knickers and straightened her skirt. She stepped outside the cubicle and automatically washed her hands. By the time she was back on the stool at the bar she was troubled because she couldn't remember the important thing that had bothered her in the toilet. She thought and thought but it wasn't coming. Too tired and too stressed she realistically appraised herself. With that she signalled the barman, dug into her handbag, found a twenty euro note, held it up to him, saw his nod, she left it on the bar and stumbled into the street. She needed home and sleep.

Chapter 15

'Six foot five and dangerous!'
'No, six foot five and highly effective!'
'Rubbish!'
'Six foot five and ....and....always right!'
'Pagh....what are you talking about?' Detective Maria Fernandez Tupelo said in exasperation as she crept into his living room and caught the end of the conversation Ferran was having with himself.
'You are six foot five and gorgeous. Any woman would want to be with you and any man would want to be you. How many other forty-five year olds could have the same said about them?'

She sat slumped in the red leather armchair facing the early morning sunlight as it streamed into his apartment. He was expressionless. He hadn't slept much that night. The day following the morning action at Gran Via had thrown him completely off kilter. He hadn't felt good about himself following his attack on Martes and, despite what his Jefe had said to him, he'd convinced himself that he was about to lose his job. The drink hadn't helped. Yesterday morning he had instantly hit a bar and drunk his favourites, a café espresso, followed by a Torres brandy shot, followed by a beer. He had been in his favourite bar in the whole world – Bar Colombo. It was positioned at the end of Passeig Joan de Borbo in Barceloneta. In the summer the bar had the best evening terrace in the whole of the city. You could sit there watching the sun go down over Port Vell and Montjuic. The rest of the year, the bar was an ordinary but welcoming haven amidst the bustle of the city. After several of these combinations the barman, Ramon, ageing but often resplendent in black leather trousers, had put him in a taxi for home, Ferran had re-directed the driver to Born and had stumbled into a cocktail bar. Numerous cocktails later and he had somehow managed to find another taxi, after stumbling down a few streets, which took him home. He now sat where he had fallen at about 3 a.m. He had slept fitfully in his brown, leather armchair, it hadn't been at all comfortable. Maria's arrival had surprised him a few minutes ago. He glanced at his watch. It was seven a.m.

'What are you playing at?' questioned Maria. She was entirely gorgeous. Late thirties, dark-haired and slim. Yet she was a detective with a passion for Detective Will Ferran. Few knew why. Maybe he too was gorgeous and intelligent.
'I'm sitting here trying to invent an image for myself. My days on the Mossos are obviously numbered, so my only future is as a private detective. That's why I need to have an image. I need to be marketable.'
'You look and sound pathetic,' she replied.
'First of all, there is no way the Mossos d'Esquadra is going to let it's finest detective go. And secondly, that thing you were just saying about being

right……you are hardly ever right…..it is the quality of the people you work with that makes you look so good.' She laughed. The last thing he felt like at that moment was laughing, Ferran felt dreadful. He had been awake for sometime, thinking about his future. His mouth and head were in unison in their rebellion against his body and his stomach was beginning to join in. The dryness of his mouth was making his throat hurt but he couldn't bear to move to get a drink of water in case he damaged his head further. He really needed the toilet now as well. Maria sensed his plight. Within seconds she had some tablets for his headache and a larger tumbler of water. She held them out in her hand.

'Here you are Will. Take these and then get yourself to the bathroom.' She smiled caringly. She was wearing expensively cut brown jeans that hugged her slender legs and rear perfectly. The brown and tan high-heeled sandals were expertly chosen to make the most of her impressive legs. Ferran, even in his desperate state, found his eyes drawn to Maria's legs.

'Why are you so gorgeous?' he croaked and put one hand on her right leg.

'Come here, you wicked woman!'

Maria moved across and sat astride Ferran. As she did so she untied the clasp that had been holding her long straight brown hair up. It fell around her face. As she put her head towards his, her hair tickled his face.

'Maria, Maria, I love you,' he said through a painful throat. She looked beautiful and he looked dreadful. An independent observer at this scene would have seen something reminiscent of 'the beauty and the beast', whereas in reality it was a situation of real tenderness between two people very much in love. Ferran held Maria's delicate shoulders as their lips melted together. They held that position for several minutes. It was the kind of kiss that said so much about how you felt about the other person. Their lips parted and they smiled as they stared into each other's eyes. Ferran then put his hand to his mouth and cupped it as he breathed heavily into his hand in order to sample his breath.

'I'm sorry, my breath……I must taste like the bottom of a bodega's cellar.'

'No matter, Will, I really enjoyed that. I haven't seen you for a couple of days.' Maria held onto his arm as she spoke. He noticed her slender fingers and their lovely colour. She was naturally slightly darker skinned than he was but she also enjoyed a couple of hours a day on the Barceloneta beaches which honed her tan to the rich brown colour on display. Maria loved jewellery and her fingers held so many gold rings that he couldn't immediately count them, but because of her passion, he was never short of an idea for a present.

'Vale. Vale. You are doing it again Maria.' He stood up and tried to look stern at her.

'I don't feel well but you are getting me aroused. Look!' He pointed at his groin with a huge smile on his face. She laughed and rolled over onto the full sofa.

'I love you Will. Why don't you marry me?'

He loved the way she said Will. It was not a natural Spanish word. She could say it but it sounded more like 'Wiyl'. Marriage though, was a scary topic. She was beautiful and he loved her, but he had been there, done that and not seen the benefits. He would love to marry Maria, but it had to be at exactly the right time. It was only five years since his very unpleasant divorce and he and Maria had only really been lovers for 18 months. He had to play this one very carefully. He didn't want to lose her.

'I love you, you gorgeous woman. Let me have a shower. Will you put some coffee on?'

Ferran used this diversionary tactic that seemed to work. She nodded glumly and headed for the kitchen whilst he crawled off to the bathroom.

Chapter 16

The coffee was brewed and smelling delightful. Maria had warmed up some croissants she had found in the fridge. All were laid out on the table in the middle of the apartment living room. The table was right next to the window that looked out onto a large terrace with a remarkable view across the city. The apartment had belonged to Ferran's mother, with whom he had lived with until she died four years ago. The only time he had ever spent away from his place was the 12 months when he was briefly, and mistakenly, married. He had lived in this apartment in Sant Gervasi all his life, overlooking the city he loved. Set, facing seaward, on Carrer de Padua, the grand apartment had been home to his father and his father's family for many years. His mother had fallen in love with Barcelona on an illicit visit to the city in the sixties. After being taken in hand by a young and savvy Senor Ferran, who protected her against the then darker side of the city, she married him, Will's father. They had all lived together very happily in the apartment for many years until first Wills' grandparents died from heart disease, within weeks of each other when they were in their eighties. Then suddenly his father, Alfonso, was killed in a hijack incident at Barcelona's El Prat Airport. He too had been a policeman. Ferran had since modernised the apartment with new fitments and new furniture, he had had nothing else to spend his money on. Maria fitted in with the expensive décor perfectly.

Ferran, feeling much refreshed and with a towel wrapped around his waist, waltzed into the living room. Maria was elegantly draped over the sofa.
'Tell me young lady?' questioned Ferran.
'Just what right do you have to treat this apartment as your home?'
Mara said nothing. She just looked at him with her brown eyes and laid back onto the sofa. As she did so, the brown silk shirt she wore strained to contain her womanhood. Ferran was on top of her like a shot. She was so gorgeous, he couldn't resist her. What he couldn't get into his head was that she felt the same about him. Maria was extremely attractive, but she was also very intelligent. She had been with many men and had been married twice. Every man she had been with had been attractive and successful but none of them could cope with her being attractive, successful and intelligent. They had all wanted an attractive woman to show off around the city. That was not for Maria. She had made real mistakes in her choice of man, but Ferran was very different. She knew he was and she wasn't going to let him get away from her. She understood him, his concerns and his demons much better than he realised.

Barcelona Betrayal

By the time they had uncoiled themselves from around each other the coffee was cold. Maria sashayed off to the kitchen to get some more.

'Will. I want to marry you,' she said as she re-entered the living room with two steaming hot cups of coffee. He was taken by surprise by this sudden statement. He thought she would have taken more notice of his earlier rebuff. Until today they had never discussed marriage.

'Why?' he queried, with an incredulous look on his face. That was all he could think of to say.

'I've been thinking a lot about you recently. I hate being away from you. We love the same things. We are both good looking and intelligent. We go very well together. We both love eating and drinking in nice places and we both love this city and the sun.....and...... I just want you.' She burst into tears and snuggled her head into his chest as she sat down next to him. Ferran was in panic. His heart was racing. His body was still in torment following his drinking the day before and now his mind had joined in. What did he think? What could he say? He didn't know what he wanted. He looked pale and confused.

'I agree with everything you just said.' The words came out of his mouth without the permission of his brain. He had a real problem with her thoughts. He didn't think he was attractive to women and he couldn't see how he could keep such a beautiful woman as Maria after the gloss had worn off for her.

'You do not, you liar,' she snapped.
'I know you very well Will Ferran Jones.'
She sat up and looked him directly in the eyes. They were no more than six inches from each other.
'You do not believe you are attractive. You think that you are just an infatuation of mine and that I will tire of you. Basically Will Ferran Jones, you think that you are not good enough for me.'
She was really fired up now. Ferran was reeling. He wasn't scared of Maria when she got into these moods, but very, very respectful. You just did not mess with her. At the same time though her passion really turned him on.
'I love you Will Ferran Jones. I have been with you now for over a year, probably nearly eighteen months, and we have a great time together. I put up with your moods as you do mine. We have both been married before and we have both been with many others, but I, and I know this is the case for you too, have never been in love like this before. You are my soul mate. Why then will you not take me as your wife?'
Ferran was in a real corner. Everything she said was right. The trouble was he had been a complete emotional mess ever since his mother had died a couple of years ago. He was alone, with the exception of Maria, and he was coping with that. His mother's death had come just after a dreadfully messy divorce which, whilst the outcome satisfied him, he had found the process very draining. For

the first time though, Maria's words were really making him think. He did love her. She was gorgeous and intelligent and they always had a great time together. Why not get married? He lay prostrate on the sofa next to Maria and put his head into her lap. She instantly softened her tone and stroked his long dark hair.

'How could I not love you Ferran? You are so soft.' She looked at him lovingly and then her expression became confused.

'But, how can you possibly be the most effective and feared detective in the Mossos?' She laughed.

Ferran looked up at her in mock hurt, then sank his head down again onto her soft lap.

'She is the most delightful of women,' he thought.

'OK, Vale.' He sat up.

'I really love you. You really love me. Let's get married.'

Ferran's words were hardly out of his mouth when Maria was hugging him and choking him with delight.

'OK, OK, that's sorted then,' he said sitting up. What had he done? His heart raced. She was delighted, but he was petrified. Maria was now sitting next to him beaming with unburdened pleasure. Her hands were curled under her chin. Ferran thought she looked like a little girl who had just won a fancy dress competition. He didn't dare tell Maria that though.

'We need to make plans for our future Maria, but let's do it later. I need to get a job first. What do you think about the Private Detective agency thing?'

'Will. What are you talking about? I have already said that you are the best detective in the Mossos and everybody knows it. What you did to Martes was perfectly justified. He had it coming to him. Jefe Perez Camps told you himself that he didn't want to lose you. He really doesn't.'

Ferran shifted on the sofa so that he was side by side with Maria. He picked up his coffee and grabbed at a croissant. She continued.

'Jefe Perez Camps gave me an official letter for you Ferran.'

She stood up and walked towards her handbag that was on the breakfast bar. She took something from inside her bag. She walked back towards him and handed him the letter. He held it. He looked at it.

'Open it.' She instructed forcibly. He didn't move, he just continued to stare at the letter as if afraid of its contents.

'It gives you authority to set up your own investigation division of the Mossos. You are being promoted to Chief Detective. I am your assistant and we are to have two of the new trainee detectives, Esteban Guillard Puyes and Jesus Serras Montenegro, with us. For our office staff we will have the wonderful Conchita and a woman who is formidably good, Gloria Buckenstock, a Spanish German who will organise you to death!'

Ferran was shocked. This was not what he had expected. He had feared the worst. He stood up and opened the letter from his Jefe. He read it carefully. The letter read exactly as Maria had said it would. The operation was to begin immediately. Ferran was to report only to Jefe Perez Camps and nobody else. They would have an office base on Via Laietana and they could call on the resources of the Mossos when required. The name of Ferran's group was the 'Special Investigations Unit' (SIU). Ferran liked that. He read the letter again. He felt much, much better. He smiled at Maria. She was delighted in every respect.

Chapter 17

This is not what she wanted. Her new life, with her new man, was meant to be idyllic. Now he wasn't there and she didn't know when she would see him again. Yesterday had been a complete washout. After the police station she had found her way home to their apartment on Carrer Maquinista and collapsed into bed. She could hear the lorries and the men at work outside emptying the large grey rubbish skips that stood on each street corner in Barceloneta. She knew it must be about 5 a.m. It was still dark outside. The apartment was on the fifth floor, the highest apartment in the building and it faced east towards the sea, although the view of the sea was hidden by several hundred metres of buildings. She always slept with the shutters and the windows open. She and Jaume liked the night noises and the cool, early-morning breezes that swept in off the sea.

She lay in bed, looking up at the ceiling. It was well decorated, like the rest of the apartment. There was a large, traditional ceiling rose in the centre of the ceiling. It was the only 'old' thing in the apartment, everything else had been modernised. As she gazed at the rose pattern she drifted off again, thinking about what had happened a couple of nights ago. She had seen what she had seen. She was now very clear about it in her mind. It had been replayed a thousand times in her mind and she knew what she had seen at the Palau Sant Jordi. The thing that she couldn't square in her head though was that, although she knew something was going to happen, she was totally surprised when it did happen. She had considered this point again and again since that night, had she simply denied that it was going to happen because she didn't want it to happen? She had agreed to the plan. That she accepted. The thing though, she kept telling herself, is that Jaume told her the actual plan in a lot of detail. In her head she could see him sitting opposite her across the white melanine table in their apartment. He had held her hands across the table and looked into her eyes earnestly as he outlined the plan. She just couldn't remember what he had said. She was very clear about the purpose, but the actual plan was nowhere to be found in her memory banks.

She remembered thinking that the plan was surreal. She recalled reflecting on this. She convinced herself that she just couldn't have been really listening when Jaume had explained it all to her. She must have been distracted. All she had wanted was a life with Jaume. She wanted to spend the rest of her life with this man, the most wonderful man she had ever met. She was totally relaxed after the ordeal of the last 36 hours. As she lay amidst the fresh brown sheets of her bed in the high-ceilinged, now sunlit room she felt her hand on her left breast. That was Jaume's favourite position. She ran her index finger around her nipple and then down to her stomach. It felt just as if Jaume was doing it. She closed her eyes and shuddered. Then her mind focussed again on the plan. The purpose of the plan, as Jaume had told it, was to make enough money to set them up for the next ten years or more. Money they could live off and invest. Jaume had little money. He was from a poor family from Navarro, in the North-West of Spain, he had few qualifications but he was improving himself. She had sold her flat in London in order to put €50,000 into the €300,000 apartment they had bought together several months ago. She loved him and they were going to get married. They would be together forever. Jaume wasn't happy with being totally financially reliant on her, he had told her. She ignored it as simply being Spanish male pride. Yet he was determined to get the money together to support them. The plan was to stage his abduction and for her to claim the insurance money. They had insured themselves for €450,000 and this could be claimed on his death. She had argued that she didn't want him dead, then she realised that he was looking at fraud. Her concern was the success of the plan. She would do anything for the love of Jaume. She told him that. She knew about the 'criteria necessary for the proof of death' though and she questioned him about how he would handle this. If there was no death certificate she knew there had to be something like a seven-year lapse before any life assurance could be claimed. Jaume had assured her. He had told her not to worry. He had thought of and planned everything. All he wanted her to do was to tell the police the truth, as she knew it. She also needed to react logically to any unusual situation. He had dwelled on this last point asking her if she understood. In the end she did. Jaume wanted her to lie if she had to.

Chapter 18

She hadn't expected things to happen so soon. She was enjoying her time with Jaume. They would walk for hours through the parks and streets of Barcelona. They loved the Ciuatadella Parc. They would sit beneath the trees enjoying the shade, arm in arm. She loved his smell and she would snuggle up to him. As she laid her head across his stomach on one of the many park benches, they would sit for hours and he would gently run his fingers through her hair. She really hadn't expected anything to happen for a month or so. He had told her the night before the concert about the plan. They had spent the evening in 'La Paradeta', the fish restaurant on Caller Comercial. Jaume loved flirting with the girls who served the fish. It was like a market stall of fresh fish. He would choose only the best seafood for her – monkfish, oysters, mussels and crab were their favourites. They sat that night eating and drinking in the busy refectory-style restaurant. They were a couple in love. The laughter eventually stopped at around ten p.m when Jaume insisted they went back to the apartment, as he had something to tell her, something he had to tell her in private.

She was still lost in her past thoughts as she crawled out of their low-lying bed. She was naked and she looked down at herself as she walked towards the bathroom. She wasn't feeling good about herself at the moment, she felt fat and bloated. In the bathroom her mirror image was surprisingly good she thought. Her hair looked good. Her thinking returned to the abduction at the Olympic Parc. It was obviously a set-up, but why did she get hurt? Her right hand felt the back of her head that was still sore. Why had the police given her a hard time? Had she performed well? She didn't know the answer. That Detective……Ferran? He was a bastard. She felt that he knew that she knew more. She didn't know any more about the abduction, yet she did know it was a set-up.

'The murder!' she shouted out aloud. 'Was it real?' The thought really scared her. What was going on?

After a while she pulled herself together, got dressed and decided that she needed caffeine. Things were better in her mind but she was still in torment. She left the apartment. In the street she headed for the Parc Estacio de Nord. To get there she had to walk though the Ciuatadella Parc and about 2 kilometres in total. It was worth it though. The little bar in the park would give her a coffee in the quiet and surreal ceramic park. She needed a quiet, different space in which to think. As she headed towards the park she was surrounded by thought. It was a twenty-minute walk from her apartment but on the way she saw, heard and noticed nothing. As she stepped through the high, iron gates of the Parc Estacio de Nord she looked up and saw a completely blue sky. It was such a shock that it momentarily took her breath away. It was as if she had never seen anything of such clear and pure beauty before. Suddenly her senses were awake. She was sure it was the influence of the park. It wasn't that big for a park. Surrounded by the Estacio de Nord, now a coach station, and tall apartments on all sides, the park was a green haven. She particularly liked the ceramic sculptures that broke up the vistas in the park. She stepped forward, enjoying the brightness. It was about eight thirty. She was relieved to see that at this time of the morning the café-bar in the park was open. It was just a brown, wooden shack set in the centre of the park. Twenty or so aluminium chairs stood starkly with several similar tables just outside the bar. She strode purposefully along the sandy, gravel track, heading for the café-bar.

Chapter 19

There were few other people around. She wasn't far from the café-bar when an old man appeared in front of her. He looked like a beggar. He surprised her. His matted hair and long, straggly beard matched perfectly his ragged clothes. He was a vagrant and stank like one. She veered away from him as he stood, steadfast, right in her path. As she scuttled away from him he shouted after her,
'You are selling your soul. I can see you are selling your soul.'
She walked on towards the café-bar, and she didn't look back. She reached the bar and asked for a coffee. Within minutes the coffee was ready. She paid, picked up the coffee and turned towards the tables. The old man had disappeared. He was nowhere to be seen.

She took a seat facing the station. Between her and the station was a jagged blue ceramic sculpture that rose out of the grass. She liked it enormously. Her mind was troubled by the image of the old vagrant and his comment. Why would he say something like that? What did he know? She felt herself getting more and more paranoid so she drank more coffee. This calmed her, although she still felt uncomfortable. It wasn't the old man. It was what he had said. She did feel like she was selling her soul by going along with Jaume's plan. She knew she would regret getting involved. The blue ceramic sculpture lay across her field of vision. The sun glistened on its edges. The sight dazzled her and she was lost in her thoughts. For a few seconds she was emotionless and relaxed, the worries that haunted her had disappeared. Suddenly she came back to reality. The sun was now higher in the clear blue sky. It was getting warm. Her mind wouldn't let go of the thoughts that had swamped her mind for the past couple of days. Yet at this moment she kept seeing the old man. His words were swimming around her head.

'You are selling your soul. I can see you are selling your soul.' Those words were ringing in her mind. She hated it. She had been deeply disturbed by the events at the Palau Sant Jordi but the old mans' words were resonating in a far more worrying way around her thoughts. Was he right? She loved Jaume, she would do anything for him, but was it right? Was this deception right? She couldn't understand why she was thinking like this. She had few moral scruples. She had done some terrible things in her short life and she was only concerned about having a good time. Why then, just when she had found her ideal man, and he wanted her, did she have concerns about lying for him? She was really confused.

'You are selling your soul. I can see you are selling your soul.' The old man's voice echoed in her mind. 'You are selling your soul. I can see you are selling your soul.' Those words kept ringing in her ears.

Barcelona Betrayal

It was a couple of hours later, mid-morning, when she eventually moved off the park seat. She was exhausted. Although she had been sitting still, she had been running everything through her mind. She had seen the old man and heard his words a thousand times. She had seen Jaume, and he looked like the old man in her mind. What then was her mind telling her? She felt deranged. Nothing seemed real. She felt absent from this world. Floating around on the fringes of reality. She was definitely feeling slightly unstable. She knew she was OK though as she was aware that she was feeling strange. It was safe to stay put. Her feelings and the games her mind was playing were taking her to dangerous places, places she didn't want to be. She was still in control at least that was what she was telling herself. The best thing to do, feeling as she did, was to sit still, stay put, and ride out the storm. Her mind churned the same thoughts over again and again in slightly different forms. Eventually she slumped in her chair, exhausted. There were only a couple of other people sitting in the chairs at the café-bar in the park. No one noticed her. To others she was just a high-powered office worker relaxing in the park. That was the impression she gave and was happy to support.

Her mind was relatively clear eventually. She stood up. She was wearing a black, cotton raincoat over her linen dress. She was very hot. The coat came off as she left the park. It hung limply over her arm as she walked across the road opposite the park. The last couple of hours had settled her mind. She was even thinking now about what she might eat for lunch. All of a sudden there was more to her life than the events of the past hours. At last she was looking forward.

Chapter 20

Via Laietana is a wide, straight road that stretches from the Port Vell on the seafront of the city to the foothills of the mountains that lie at the west of the city. The road was built a couple of centuries ago as a very necessary airway for the city, to open up the old, medieval streets. Ferran looked down on the busy street below. The Hotel Suizo was directly opposite and between where he stood and the hotel was one of the busiest parts of the city. The area he was looking over was the natural route through to the Cathedral Square and the Plaça Jaume 1. People ambled here and there. Others stood considering their next move. Some even risked crossing the busy road without the help of the green man. Ferran didn't care about what anyone else was doing, when he found himself in the centre of the hubbub of the city he was entranced by the noise and the bustle. He loved his city. He loved the vibrancy of it. He always wanted to be in the heart of it.

The offices of the Special Investigations Unit (SIU) were very grand. They were not big. Three rooms. It was formerly an apartment, a grand high-ceilinged apartment. The team were getting things sorted. All the equipment was installed and the place was just about operational. The team were all there. Maria stood at the entrance to the offices. She leant against the doorframe. She always reflected the fashions of the moment. She was resplendent in a red, tartan trouser suit and a short red woollen jacket. Whatever she wore she looked really classy. To Ferran she looked like a twenty million peseta woman at any time, but today she looked stunning. He tried not to look at her. What he really wanted to know was something that had really fascinated him these past eighteen months. How did she manage to put on the amount of make-up that she wore so quickly and to make it look so good every day. She spent even less time in the bathroom than he did. She went in make-upless and came out transformed each morning. Not that she looked at all bad without make-up, it was just that make-up took her looks to another level.

Conchita helped him to focus his mind elsewhere. He could see her animated actions a few metres away. She talked almost non-stop, not in an annoying way at all but with enthusiasm and intelligence which always made her interesting. The better Ferran knew her the more he liked her way of thinking. She knew something about everything and had an opinion, which was well-informed, about most things. Conchita Pedralbes Carew was a tall, black-haired graduate of Montevideo University. To look at she was the kind of woman that any man would want but the kind that any man would forget. Men immediately saw an attractive woman who was strong-willed and intelligent. She scared them off. Her personality, though, was infectious. She laughed and she talked incessantly. She was totally uninhibited. She was a delight to be with. She was extremely clever and, in Ferran's view, the most thorough researcher he had ever met. They had a mutual professional love for each other. He loved her for her completeness. He had never met anyone so intelligent with such an engine and with such a vibrant personality. She was fun, clever and great to look at. She loved him because he had been the only person who had believed in her when she first joined the Mossos. She also thought he was gorgeous, although she loved the fact that her great friend Maria was getting it together with Ferran.

Chapter 21

Maria assumed control of the office. She was officially Ferran's deputy in the SIU but in reality she was the organisational brain. Ferran was the deep thinker, the ideas man, the intuitive detective. Maria was his perfect foil. She was excellent with people, very thorough and highly organised. She was perfect in every respect for Ferran. She organised him and she made sure that he covered all bases. She swept up behind him and picked up the pieces and she tried to look ahead and smooth the pathways ahead of him. She was not only great to work with but she had very high standards.
'Are you going to sit there and let the women do all the setting up of this office Esteban? Even Jesus is trying to get the fax machine operating. What are you doing?' she complained, as she stared questioningly at Esteban Guillard Puyes. He was in his mid twenties and straight out of University. A top graduate, a good brain, he had a real personality but he appeared, to her, to lack initiative. His fresh-faced look was out of place in his deep blue suit and cream shirt. He looked very young.
'Sorry, Detective Fernandez Tupelo, I was just looking at the cases we have been given to work on'.
Maria's face softened to a smile.
'OK, Esteban, that is a very useful thing to do. But, you must call me Maria.'

Barcelona Betrayal

He smiled to himself and looked at his knees, almost embarrassed by the personal attention he was getting from this beautiful woman. He went back to the computer screen and continued his work.

Across the other side of the main room was the other young detective who was part of the team, Jesus Serras Montenegro. He was on his back looking up into the rear of a huge, antiquated fax machine. His long, black hair and goaty beard lent him a typical Spanish look, appearing like a young Antonio Banderas. Above him, pressing buttons and banging all parts of the machine, was the final member of the SIU team. The detectives were excellent but without a sound administrator they would be nothing. The final member of the team was the formidably good Gloria Buckenstock. She was striking looking. Nearly six foot tall, pure blonde hair, resting short cropped on top of a bronzed, toned super-fit body. She had been national champion at 800 metres for Spain for many years and was expected to win gold at her home Olympics, in Barcelona in 1992. She pulled up injured in the heats and retired from athletics soon after. That was nearly 15 years ago. She had kept herself fit. Very fit. She was also very good at her job. Her mother was Spanish and her father had been German. The marriage of a flamenco dancer and a world quality athlete had, to her, been a blessing, although everyone else thought it was the reason for her sexual confusion. Gloria was determinedly single. She was always going to do what she wanted to do. She lived alone and always had. Her temperament and attitude to life meant that she could not tolerate sharing her life with anyone. Yet she liked company and was very good socially with people. She was nearing fifty now, but she looked much younger. She was very attractive, with long legs, firm breasts and a good figure. Although she didn't want permanent company she liked sex. She was quite regimented in her life and she had to have sex twice a week. She used it as part of her fitness regime. By all accounts she was also extremely good at sex. A session with Gloria lasted well over an hour and was very physical. She didn't mind if she had sex with a man or a woman, although she needed an injection of something that only a man could provide at least once a month. She had a regular group of lovers who were happy to have sex with her on her demand whenever she wanted it, but with no ties. But she had a real taste for people. She had tried to get Maria and Conchita into her bed, but both had made it very clear to her that they were not interested in that side of things at all. So she had left them alone. Ferran had been a regular target, despite his rejections. He had been tempted, but he was also scared of her physically, so he had always managed to reject her advances. She now knew about him and Maria and, as she was not into breaking up a perfect partnership, she also left him alone. Her manner with Jesus at the fax machine made it obvious what she was having for a meal that evening.

Chapter 22

Ferran strolled back from the window and surveyed his team and the offices.

'OK. Team meeting.'

With that they all stopped what they were doing and ambled off to a smaller adjoining room where there was a rectangular red oak table with eight black leather chairs surrounding it. The furniture filled the room. They all sat down. Esteban held a file of the cases given to the SIU that he had printed off from the computer.

'What have we got then Esteban? We need to get working,' Ferran barked. He leant back on his chair at the head of the table. The others all looked towards the young detective. He replied with assurance.

'Three cases. One, a situation at Sant Cugat, some company director is suspected of siphoning off a lot of his companies money.'

Ferran raised his eyebrows to the ceiling.

'Wow, they are giving us some really interesting cases.' He exhaled in exasperation.

'It does look interesting Detective Ferran. The Mossos has taken this a long way and they believe that there are links to people smuggling from Africa,' replied Esteban.

'Yes.' Giving a stern look towards Ferran.

'We've got to remember that we are the Special Investigations Unit and we will not get any cases that are routine,' interjected Maria. Ferran looked suitably chastised and signalled with his eyes towards the young detective to continue. Esteban looked around at the faces of the others and then returned to his papers.

'The second case, is the disappearance of a Spanish citizen and the report of an unconfirmed murder at the Palau Sant Jordi. This looks....'

'I've already been involved in this one,' Ferran snapped.

'It is not going anywhere. I don't like or believe the English woman involved. Why has Jefe Perez Camps given us this one?'

Esteban looked back at the case file.

'It says here that the detectives investigating the case could not find any evidence of abduction or of the reported attempted murder, but they have real suspicions that this might be a case involving serious fraud. It is definitely an interesting one.'

Esteban glowed with enthusiasm, although he was aware of his boss's negative attitude towards the case. Ferran smiled.

'I applaud your keenness Esteban, tell us about the other case.'

'There have been three, apparently unrelated, murders in the Horta area of the city, all look like marital disputes but they have all happened in the past year.'

The six of them sat around looking at each other for a few minutes. No one spoke. The traffic outside the room continued to hum and rumble.

Ferran was lost in his thoughts. Suddenly he leant forward and put his hands flat on the table.

'What do you all think? It looks to me as if the most difficult case at first sight is going to be the missing person. What do you all think? Maria?' He looked to her sitting on his left.

'I don't know. It is certainly worth spending some time digging. The Horta case looks co-incidental to me at first sight, and I agree with you Ferran about the level of interest in the Sant Cugat case.' Maria was relaxed about the whole thing. No-one else was bothered either.

'OK. This is what we will do.' Ferran stood up. He loved all this. For the first time in his career he had been given some real freedom. He no longer had to work with a bunch of loser detectives and cow-tow to their whims. He had been given an opportunity. This was his chance, this was what his life had been missing, some real responsibility. He wasn't going to make a mess of this. He wanted to be democratic and build a team, but he also knew he had to lead. He had a reputation to uphold. They all knew he was a great detective, but could he share his skills with others? Could he lead a team? This was a real test.

'We will work all the cases together but each of us will take the lead on one particular case. Maria, I want you to look into the Sant Cugat situation, but first could you interview the English woman involved in this abduction? Against my better judgment I will take the lead on this case but I think she may open up more to a woman.' He paused and walked across to the huge window that also looked out across the busy Via Laietana.

'Esteban and Jesus you two will share the Horta killings. I do think that we will find no connection there between the various murders, but I may be wrong.' He looked across at the two young detectives. They were obviously pleased with the responsibility they had been given.

Conchita. You are the best investigative researcher in the world.' He smiled at her. She blushed through her dark skin.

'You really need to find out as much as you can about this businessman in Sant Cugat. Also, could you look into the abductions, missing people and murders over the past ten years in the city and see if there are any links with this guy the Englishwoman at Palau Sant Jordi has reported being abducted.' With that he threw down a picture of Jaume Reyes Lugano. Conchita picked it up.

'What about the Horta murders? Do you want me to find some information? Anything?'

'Conchita, if there is anything, you will find it. Look for it,' insisted Ferran.

'Let's go.'

With that statement they all stood up and headed out of the room.

'Meet here and report back at 8.30 a.m tomorrow,' shouted Ferran. He watched them all flow out of the room and stream off towards their separate locations. This was real police work and this was a real police force. He loved it. He put his hands on the deep windowsill and looked out over the busy street below. Within minutes he saw Esteban and Jesus racing through the crowded pavements. He sighed. He remembered the feeling, the rush of excitement. They both had the capacity to be excellent detectives. He vowed there and then to train them well. His sight was caught by a striking vision. A woman full of sophistication and poise strolled though the busy scene. The woman looked like she was superimposed onto the street scene. He was captivated by her poise and her presence. It was Maria. He shot back from the window. He wiped his forehead. He knew she was the one. How could he, a man in control of his emotions, be so besotted with a woman? He knew he was totally in love with her.

Chapter 23

Life slowly began to return to normal. At least it felt normal. Normal, though, felt empty. She was getting used to being alone in this foreign city. She had loved the city that was the home of her lover, Barcelona. Alone though, she still wasn't sure how she felt about the place. She loved many parts of the city although the romance just wasn't there without him. Gradually though she had begun to explore the city and found places she had never discovered before. She became more aware and less dependent on Jaume. She couldn't rely on him any more as he wasn't there. Her language skills were improving. Slowly she was assuming a life of her own in the city. She was actually beginning to enjoy herself. She knew no one. She didn't have a job and she had no contact with anyone, but she could see a way ahead for herself.

The beach was deserted. The long promenade stretched from Barceloneta, past the Hospital del Mar, down to the Olympic Port. It was a good mile walk along the grey-paved promenade. She explored the rectangular slates that were laid fifty thick across the walkway. Her head was down. Occasionally she looked up at the grey sea and at the beach. The sea breeze was cool and the weather was very damp. It wasn't raining but it had been and more looked likely. This wasn't a day for the beach. August was a good month in Barcelona for sun worshippers, but not today. She walked and walked.

In front of the hospital she decided to turn around and head back towards the Barceloneta barrio. Why, she didn't know. Maybe she had gone far enough. She had exercised her mind in the fresh, damp air. She felt revived. Her mind was ready to open up to new experiences. It felt cleansed like a reformatted hard drive. It felt re-conditioned. All around her was the sight of people in wheelchairs being exercised from the hospital that sat opposite her. Nurses and attendants were smiling and joking with a wide range of patients. She hadn't really noticed the large hospital before, yet she had regularly walked this way with Jaume. It was a great location for a hospital. She saw the people immobile in their wheelchairs, dependent on their helpers. The sight of these people instantly helped her to feel released. She had been dependent. Her infatuation with Jaume had, she suddenly realised, been claustrophobic, limiting and restricting. She had been trapped in a wheelchair called life. Suddenly she realised how lucky she was. She stood up straight and a very clear thought came into her head.

'Time for a beer.' She smiled fortuitously to herself. She was walking on the balls of her feet now. The deep-rooted slump, the way she had been holding herself recently, was replaced by a springy step. Before long she was sitting at a table, clothed in blue plastic, outside Daguiri on the Barceloneta seafront. All the tables were empty, which was unusual. She told herself it was the weather that was still looking threatening and was putting people off from risking an outside seat. She didn't care. Let it rain. After a few minutes a waitress appeared reluctantly. She ordered a beer and the salad of the day that was always good at this place. The beer came first. She took a sip.

Chapter 24

'Sandie.'

A voice came from the table behind her. She hadn't noticed anyone there when she had sat down. She ignored the sound.

'Sandie.'

This time she sat up. She definitely heard it.

'Sandie, do not look around.'

She froze. What was happening? How did a total stranger sitting behind her know her?

'I have a message from Jaume,' the voice said.

She froze. She had almost forgotten about him. Her body melted as her recollections of Jaume and her love for him re-acquainted themselves with her mind. In an instant she found herself fantasising about the special sex they had. Sitting at a table at Daguiri on the sea front at Barceloneta she suddenly had a vision of her lover Jaume standing above her with a toreador's hat on his head and a silver and gold toreador's jacket around his shoulders. Apart from these adornments he was naked. His manhood was more than erect and they were about to have sex. He loved this ritual. It was his party piece with her. He loved to take the macho role and it made him feel strong, powerful and in control. She didn't care about what he wanted from it, because she absolutely loved it.

'Jaume is OK,' the voice said quietly. She snapped her mind back into focus.

'I need to see him, I want to see if he is alright,' she pleaded.

'Is he OK? How is he coping without me? Tell me how he is managing.'

There was no reply from behind her. She stopped speaking and slowly turned to look behind her. The sun was streaming down through the stormy clouds. A ray of light fell onto the pavement right outside the entrance to the Daguiri bar. But there was no one there. She looked around for people who were walking away from the scene, but there was no one there. Her eyes scanned everything within twenty yards, but there was no one in sight. She glanced back at the seat that had supported the source of the voice, hoping that someone would be there. There was nobody there. As her eyes viewed the table again she leapt forward instinctively as she glimpsed a rectangular white envelope propped upright on the table against an empty beer glass. She could see her name written on it.

'Sandie.' It was written in Jaume's scribble.

The envelope rested in the palm of her hand. She looked at it. It was contact. Her initial elation had left her like air leaves a balloon, quickly and decisively. She felt strange. The feeling of independence that was creeping into her mind was nice. She was just feeling free and relaxed. It was almost a disappointment that Jaume was back in her life. She couldn't believe how she was feeling. Thoughts raced around her head. Was he just an

infatuation? Maybe she was just depressed and he had simply given her the attention she craved? Perhaps she didn't love him after all? She was shocked with herself for thinking such thoughts.
'Pull yourself together woman,' she shouted to herself.
She ripped open the letter.

My love Sandie,

I can only wonder how you must feel at this moment. My heart feels broken, as you are not by my side. I would do anything to be with you, although I know that what I have done will help us be together forever.

I am sure you were your usual strong and helpful self with the Mossos, following my disappearance. You must be very careful. They will investigate and possibly even follow you. For this reason we must not meet for six months. I know this is a dreadful thought. I have a picture of you in my pocket. I carry it near my heart. We cannot even speak on a mobile as the calls can be traced. You must be strong and look after the apartment.

Shortly the Mossos will ask you to identify someone. You must agree with their assumptions. This is an important part of the plan.

Be strong Sandie.
I love you.

The letter was signed, *Jaume.*

She sat in the aluminium chair outside Daguiri. The rain started to fall sporadically. She didn't move. The letter was pegged between her index finger and the thumb of her right hand that hung limply from her arm that rested on the side of the seat. She stared towards the sea. A few people scuttled along the Passeig de Maritim, the seafront. The space her head was in, at that moment, was quite surreal. It felt as if she was a casual observer hovering ten feet above herself, looking at two very different people. The one on the left was lost. She was beside herself with grief. It was as if someone had died. The one to the right was confused, thinking about what it all meant and was very disturbed that the letter meant nothing to her. As she hovered above her two selves she found herself looking for the self she preferred. It was difficult. It was a very difficult choice. Did she want the man of her dreams....eventually? The man she loved, or so she thought. The man who always supported her? The man she could spend the rest of her life with. Or alternatively, did she want a life where she was in control, strong, confident and growing as a person? She hovered in her thoughts for quite some time.

The rain continued to patter. The drops were huge but infrequent. A large drop landed on her nose. She lost the vision for a second, but she had already decided which Sandie she wanted. In those few lost seconds she had seen the future of Sandie Shaw. She did love Jaume and she wanted him for the rest of her life, but it was going to be on her terms. If he didn't like that then maybe he wasn't the man for her. She had realised through all her deliberations over recent days that their relationship was destroying her, not, as she had thought, supporting her. Jaume had squeezed the confidence out of her. She now realised that. He had brought her onto his territory and made her dependent on him. These thoughts did not change her feelings for him. She was pleased to hear from him at last. Her love for him was as strong as ever, but he would have to contend with a different woman in six months time. She liked her mind's revelations of the past few days. It had performed an amazing trick and had totally redirected her life. All of a sudden she knew who she was and what she wanted from life. The rain had stopped. The waitress dashed across to her with her salad. She ordered another beer and relaxed into her lunch.

Chapter 25

Will Ferran knew that he was on fire, he felt totally energised. The past few months had been challenging. He had lost his way and he had been questioning his life. All that was now a long way behind him. Right now he had a new role, a great team and the prospect of an amazing new wife. He felt good.

'You are six foot five and gorgeous. Any woman would want to be with you and any man would want to be you.' He ran Maria's words through his head. He wasn't vain but those words made him feel really fine. As he walked along Via Laietana towards the bay where his car was parked he tried to catch his image in the shop windows. He was just checking himself out. His shopping spree with Maria last night had also added to his feel-goodness. She had style and taste. His own taste wasn't so bad, but he, like most men, lacked the confidence of their own choices in relation to clothes. He often dumbed down, buying something that was safe rather than slightly different, and Ferran did like to be a little different. He liked to skirt the edges of acceptability. He never followed the norm. Even at school he would be into some weird way-out music that he liked to tell people about. Invariably though, the bands he liked always made it big. His judgment was excellent. His clothes though, they were something else. He loved clothes. He had little else to spend his money on. By himself he would buy black. He felt it complemented his long, straight, black hair. He thought in his own mind that he looked like the rock singer Bryan Ferry. He looked nothing like him in reality, but Ferran felt like him. Sometimes when he had this conversation with people about his perceived likeness to the singer, he reflected as to whether or not he was actually gay, perhaps he actually fancied the man! Within seconds of thinking these kind of thoughts his macho genes always fired in and alerted him to the fact that anything that was slim, tanned and ample-breasted with a gorgeous rear always, without question, aroused his manhood. He had convinced himself several years ago that his infatuation with Bryan Ferry was as an icon, an icon of style.

Chapter 26

Yesterday his woman, he loved that term, had asked him to marry her. His woman. He could say that again and again. He liked even more the idea of calling her his wife. That was a real step forward. His previous wife had been nice and he had loved her for a few months, but it had been a mistake. Maria, though, was way beyond the average man. She knew it and he knew it. Her man had to be equal to her. He had to be intelligent, handsome, special and different. There were not many men like that around. Maria knew it, in all her thirty-eight years she had only ever met one man that met all her needs and she really loved him, Will Ferran Jones. He dwelt on the fact that she really adored him. He checked off the criteria. Intelligent: yes, he could accept that, he was very good at his job. Special: true, he was the best detective in the Mossos. He had been told this many times so it must be true. Different: yes, he had spent his whole forty-five years ensuring that there was only one Will Ferran and that he was totally unique. Interesting: definitely. He was destined one day, he believed, to be a great thriller writer. Move over Montalban, Ferran was next in line. He wrote for pleasure, but one day, one day, he would get himself published and take his writing to a far more serious level. The one criterion that troubled him was the handsome one. He was very confident in his ability, always had been. The idea that he was handsome or good-looking was really his Achilles' heel. He behaved with a real lack of confidence around women. They always loved his strength, his intelligence and the fact that he was different, but he always lost it on the confidence front. Maria though, saw through him totally. To her he was the most handsome man in the world.

Ferran was troubled by his appearance. Maria told him all the time that he was gorgeous and that he turned her on. He just couldn't see it. He spent hours looking in mirrors and trying to catch his reflection in shop windows in an attempt to see what it was that she loved. No joy though. He couldn't get in line with her thinking. She could see deeply inside him though. She was styling him. Maria had known Ferran for eighteen months. In that time he had lost a stone in weight. He was eating less, but drinking more. He was longer-haired and dressing more appropriately.

Last night had been the best night ever for shopping. Ferran quite enjoyed shopping, but Maria was an Olympic champion at it. Last night Ferran had hit the level of elation that he supposed most women hit quite regularly when shopping. They had visited the store of Adolfo Domingez in the Born area of the city. They had gone to the same shop in the Maremagnum and on the Passeig de Gracia, but the shop on Carrer Ribera was really something else. It was on a residential street opposite the Ciuatadella Parc and almost directly facing the huge iron structure of Born Market in its ongoing stages of refurbishment. It was not the kind of shop that anyone would normally, just casually go into. The building housing the shop was quite superb in its layout and atmosphere. Architectural fashion was the only way that Ferran could describe his shopping experience. The building from the outside is one of the typical, grand, regency style apartment blocks that frame the city. The apartments are high-ceilinged, each with tall, brown shutters across their floor to ceiling windows. As you walk into the building you quickly realise that there are two floors, as a huge set of black steel stairs descend into the basement. Ancient brickwork is exposed and there are acres of space. The spacious feel and the almost timeless, unhurried, atmosphere was what really grabbed his attention. Ferran found himself eulogising about the store, not just because of the great designs but also to because of the experience that the shop provided.

That night Ferran had picked up a couple of classy, short-sleeved shirts and a wonderful linen jacket for less than half price. They had been shopping primarily for Ferran but Maria couldn't resist the sales. She picked up an embroidered dress at a quarter of the original price. When she tried on the dress Ferran nearly collapsed with frustration. She looked so beautiful all he wanted to do was fuck her. He couldn't and that was really hard. He really couldn't believe the relationship the two of them had.

Chapter 27

Ferran turned the key in the ignition of his white Seat Cordoba. It wasn't a great looking car. Maybe once, but now it was battered and a poor example of Spanish ergonomics. It fired up immediately and he put it onto the route towards Montjuic. He was heading towards Palau Sant Jordi. He was looking for clues. He needed to see for himself if there was anything reliable from the report provided by the English woman. It was a couple of days later and forensics had combed the area but he needed to see it for himself. The white Seat powered on towards the Olympic Parc. It wasn't long before Ferran was pacing around at the side of the Palau Sant Jordi, around the car park and the traders entrance. He stood still and looked up at the balcony of the concert hall above him. He also noticed the floodlit sports park that lay, just two hundred metres, to his left.

Maria rammed her foot onto the brake of her Volkswagon Beetle Cabriolet. It was yellow and very high profile. There were no parking places along Carrer Maquinista but she pulled up on the pavement and placed her police parking permit on the windscreen. She got out of the car and looked up and down the street. Today she was looking businesslike. Her hair was tied up. She wore toned down jewellery and a plain trouser suit that almost made her blend into the background. As soon as she had got her bearings she headed towards her destination. Within a few minutes she was ringing the bell to the apartment of Sandie Shaw.

The tarmac that covered the car park had a freshly washed look. There was nothing there for Ferran to pick up on. He looked inside the rubbish skips. Nothing. Clean, for skips, but nothing to support the reported observation. He stood in the middle of the small car park frustrated. There was nothing. He ran his right hand through his hair. He had had a feeling that he was going to find something significant. That was why he was here. He was dependent on his intuition. It wasn't working the way he had expected, and he was really starting to doubt himself. The place was clean. He really was disappointed. He walked in each direction, questioning everything he was doing. He was about to head off to his Seat when he noticed a hedge at the edge of the main car park bay. The hedge was thick and uncared for. Ferran had no idea what type of plant the hedge was. All he knew was that it was green and very thick. Ferran walked over to the hedge. He looked inside its leaves, branches and between the weeds that flooded the earth at the base of the plant. He reached inside the hedge. His hand connected immediately with the thing his eyes had seen. He pulled his arm slowly out of the hedge to avoid getting scratched. He stood up straight and held an empty 'Red Line Oil' plastic container in his hand. Ferran stared at it for a second or two. The label wasn't that weather worn, so it hadn't been in the hedge for long. It was an unusual thing to find at any location as the make of oil certainly wasn't Spanish and he couldn't ever remember seeing the make before. The top was still on the container. He twisted it off and peered down the neck of the bottle container. He couldn't see much, but the liquid that was still in the bottle was red. He poured it out. A few red drips of thick oil slopped onto the ground. It was weird stuff this oil. It looked like shiny blood.

Within seconds Ferran was onto the Mossos forensics team. He called them back out to the scene. He knew what had happened. He was actually beginning to believe her story. It was clear all of a sudden to him that she had really seen what had looked like a murder. This bottle of oil just couldn't have been left here by chance. If the oil had been spread out to look like blood, from a distance, it would have looked very realistic. The advantage of using the oil was that in a car park no one would be surprised to find oil. Ferran knew there was much more evidence in this area than had been found so far. In his mind he was pleased that his internal radar was still working.

There was no one in the apartment. Maria had tried ringing the outside bell to the fifth floor apartment but there had been no answer. She had then waited for a resident and had eventually been

let into the block. Several minutes of knocking on the apartment door had convinced her that there was no one home. She had skipped down two floors when suddenly she had to grab hold of the banister firmly to stop her crashing into someone. She was inches away from a young woman. Instantly she knew who it was.
'Sandie Shaw?' questioned Maria.
The woman in front of Maria stared at her blankly. She looked at her in shock. She was thinking.
'Who is this beautiful woman? Do I know her? What is she doing in my apartment block?' Her questions were soon answered.
'Maria Fernandez Tupelo, Detective, Mossos d'Esquadra. Are you Sandie Shaw?' There was a firmness in her voice.
'Yes.' Quivered the woman.
'Can I speak to you? Let's go to your apartment,' instructed Maria. Together they staggered up to the apartment and Sandie Shaw put her key into the door in order to let them in. The door opened into a white apartment. Everything in the hallway was white. The two women strolled into the main living room of the flat. It wasn't big but it was light, airy and opened up onto a balcony. The sun was streaming through the open window. The living room was white. The whiteness of the room was broken up by the presence of two small, brown suede sofas. Maria sat down on one. Sandie Shaw stayed on her feet.
'Do you want a drink?'

'No, I just want to ask you a few questions in relation to the incident you reported earlier this week.'

'Oh. That. Yes, I will tell you what I know, although I have been through all this once.'

'I know but I think there is more to say.' Maria was firm and professional. She needed to control the conversation but also needed to appear honest and receptive.

'Tell me, where do you think Jaume is?'

She looked surprised by the question. She quickly composed herself and thought carefully about her answer.

'I think he is in Valencia, or Madrid, or Valladolid. ....come on ...I have no idea. But I want him here.' She paused and looked tearful.

'Jaume is strong and wherever he is, he is OK,' she pouted.

'I really don't want to go though all this now detective. Could we arrange to meet in a few days? I am still coming to terms with the whole thing.'

Maria could see that there was very little that she was going to get out of her at this moment in time. She opted for the easiest route.

'OK, here is my card. I need to see you within the next couple of days. Phone me.'

Chapter 28

The sun was high and hot. The tarmac around the delivery area to the Palau Sant Jordi was steaming. The forensic team was sweltering in their white protective suits. It was hot, slow, painstaking work. Ferran was sat on a grass verge. He still had his jacket on but he had taken his tie off and unbuttoned his white shirt at the top. The conversation he was having on his mobile was useful. In the past couple of hours whilst he had been with the forensics team Detectives Esteban Guillard Puyes and Jesus Serras Montenegro, of his SIU, had been out to Horta to investigate the series of marital murders. There had actually been four separate murders within an area of about five square kilometres within the past 12 months, with three committed in the past 6 months. It was very unusual to find such a cluster of murders, and even more unusual when the exact nature of the murders was closely examined. In each case the woman had been badly beaten up before being stabbed with a kitchen knife. The two young detectives had only made preliminary enquiries and had much more work to do, but their instinct, however underdeveloped, had immediately told them that the crimes were unrelated. Three of the murder scenes had had the bodies of the husbands there, after they had taken their own lives, suggesting that they themselves had murdered their partners. The fourth murder was an unusual one. The woman was an Englishwoman in her early thirties and there was no sign of the murderer and few clues. The local Mossos had already spent a great deal of time on this particular case and had come up with nothing at the time of the initial investigation. The husband, an anaesthetist at a local hospital, had been in Madrid training for several weeks at the time of his wife's death. To Detective Serras Montenegro the description the police had developed from neighbours of the husband sounded, like the description of the man abducted at the Palau Sant Jordi. Ferran, on hearing this, had immediately phoned Conchita who fed the information into the computer. Some minutes later it came up with the fact that the Englishwoman murdered in Horta had reported the disappearance of her husband 12 months before. However, he had turned up a week or so later, claiming that he had left as the result of an argument. The subsequent investigation found that he had in reality, been with another Englishwoman. Someone he had met whilst training in London earlier in the year. The parallels with the case Ferran was working on were interesting. Ferran's brain was working overtime. He was on the phone to Maria who was heading up to Sant Cugat talking through what the young detectives had discovered and finding out how her visit to the Englishwoman had gone.

'Yes, yes, I think you're right. That is what we need to do. I will finish up here and we will meet back at

the SIU office later this evening. Enjoy Sant Cugat.'
He smiled at her reply, which was quite rude.
Despite this they had a very thorough and
professional relationship at work.

Chapter 29

'Detective Ferran, we have done all we can do for now. There are a number of things we need to look at back at the lab, but we have been pretty successful in surveying the area,' commented the Chief of the forensics team, Gabriel Baptista.
'I really can't understand why the previous forensics team didn't find all this. It was Jorge Morientes. His team. He is sloppy, no good, and much too friendly with your friend Martes,' he said ironically. He smiled supportively at Ferran.
'News travels fast in the Mossos,' the detective thought to himself. He felt mildly embarrassed by this open display of support. He quickly moved the conversation on.
'What have you found then?' asked Ferran getting to his feet. Baptista was a short man, with a totally shaved head. Ferran dwarfed him. Facing each other they could have been examples of two totally different species of creature.
'There was evidence of the red oil on the ground around the skip. Some form of detergent has been used to clean it up. But there are residues.'
'How long has it been there?' quizzed Ferran
'Not long and it seems to match the oil in the bottle. We will test that. It was a good idea to use the red oil. In the darkness it would have looked like blood and there would only be traces of motor oil on the tarmac, something you could expect in a car park,' justified Baptista. He was removing his

white cover suit as he spoke. The sweat was pouring off him.

'We also found a number of fingerprints on the skip. Some will almost certainly be those of the rubbish collectors but we are hoping that there will be some other interesting matches. We found various other things in the bushes which we need to test in order to find any matching fingerprints.'

'Good work Gabriel, keep me informed.' Ferran patted Baptista on the shoulder and headed off into the Palau Sant Jordi through the delivery entrance. He had earlier asked for a record of the guards on duty the night of the alleged murder. The list of names was now ready. He checked them against the guards interviewed by the Mossos detectives on the night of the incident. There was one guard on duty that wasn't on the list of those interviewed. His name was Jose Muttaner. Ferran asked the office administrator for his address. He took it on a printed piece of paper and headed off immediately in his white Seat.

Chapter 30

The guard lived only a few streets away in Carrer Rados. Within minutes he was outside an apartment building reaching five storeys high. It was a nice area, right next to a theatre and within a short walk of the Olympic Parc. He rang the buzzer to the apartment.
'What?' Came a gruff, deep voice, almost instantly.
'Detective Ferran, Mossos d'Esquadra. Can I speak to you, please Senor Muttaner.'
'Si, no problem.'
He came down to Ferran and opened the apartment door.
'Can we talk outside? My wife is a nurse and she is on night shift at the moment. She is upstairs asleep.'
'Yes of course. I will not keep you long.'
Muttaner was young and rangy in his appearance. He had an intelligent and respectful look about him. Ferran liked him instantly. He wasn't fazed by Ferran at all. He was relaxed and listened intently to the detective.
'Can you remember being on duty at the Palau Sant Jordi a few days ago in the evening. It was the night of the Red Hot Chilli Peppers concert?'
'Yes, I remember it well.'
'Why is that?'
'Well the concert was superb.' He smiled, running the memory through his head.

'Do you work there often? Are you a regular? Would you remember one particular night?' fired Ferran.

'I am a student at the University, but I work as a guard at the Palau on occasions, usually when good bands are on.' He looked at Ferran.

'I get in for free, the work is easy and it's good pay.'

Ferran was enjoying the conversation. The sun was shining and Muttaner was willing to answer anything.

'Are you at University in Barcelona?'

'Si.'

'Studying what?'

'Literature. Catalan literature.'

Ferran was now fully engaged.

'I would have loved to have studied literature.'

'Oh. Why?' replied a slightly bemused Muttaner, unsure suddenly about the direction the conversation was now taking.

'I studied criminal psychology, but I love writing. I want to write more.'

'What's your style….your genre?'

'Thrillers, detective thrillers.'

'Montalban!'

'Si.'

'Great. I want to write like Marsé.'

They both laughed.

'Interesting, but let's get back to the detective work,' corrected Ferran.

'What do you remember about the night of the Chilli's concert? Anything?'

'Well yes, I do remember something, but it was very strange.'
'What?' Ferran was refocused on his mission and listening intently.
'There was this Englishwoman who was in a state of shock when I spoke to her.'
'Why, what had happened?'
'Well, she was on the balcony outside and she was white as a sheet. She claimed to have seen someone murdered. She seemed very confused and spacey, so there was little I could do for her.'
'Did you see anything? Did you see anything suspicious?'
'Not at all, there was no one or nothing in the area she was pointing to.'
'Are you absolutely sure?' Ferran was frustrated by the answer. He swept his long black hair back in frustration with his right hand. He left his hand flat of his forehead. His eyes focussed on the ground whilst he thought about his next question. Jose Muttaner was dressed in a blue world cup T-shirt and a pair of black shorts. He leant against the doorframe looking casually at the detective.

Eventually, Ferran looked up at the student guard.
'OK. I want you to really picture what you thought and what you saw that night. How was the Englishwoman behaving? Was there anything on the ground down in the delivery bay? Things like that.'
It was Muttaner's turn to look thoughtful.

'I really cannot remember seeing anything down in the delivery bay. There was someone walking near the cars some 50 metres away but there was no body on the ground.'

'What did the person look like?'

'It was very dark and the figure was dressed darkly, it was walking quickly away from the Palau. I didn't think it had anything to do with what the lady was talking about. All she was saying was that there was a body.'

'You said it was moving, was it a man or woman?'

'Very hard to tell. It wasn't a big figure and if it was a man he wasn't tall. If I had to choose I would say it was a woman.'

Ferran was very interested in this comment.

'The English woman, how was she behaving?'

'Very weird. To tell you the truth, I was a little scared of what she might do.'

'Weird. How?'

'She was too anguished by what she had seen. It was as if she was already really troubled by something and then, seeing something terrible, it tipped her completely over the edge.'

'Did you believe her when she said she had seen a murder and a body?'

'Yes, I think she did see something.'

Ferran had taken this conversation as far as he could. He thanked Jose Muttaner for his time and went back to his car. Ferran was pleased with this information, but he had plenty of thinking to do. He started up the Seat and it squealed away from his parking place. As he drove he phoned each one of his team asking them to meet him back at the SIU offices at 6 p.m.

Chapter 31

Conchita was sitting at her desk in the office, drumming her fingers on the oak desktop. She looked good. Her eyes were alive. They were emerald green and striking. Her dark skin merged into her brown shirt and brown jeans. She kept looking up at the door, waiting for someone.

'For goodness sake Conchita, he is on his way. Just wait. I am very sure that your information can hold,' scolded Gloria

'I have found out some great information. Ferran is going to love it.' The words spewed out of her mouth. She loved working for him. He really respected and valued her talents and had always told her so. He was great at third person affirmations, always making sure that other people knew how brilliant Conchita was at her work, often telling them in front of her. It made her feel ten feet tall. Ferran was clever. He really did think she was brilliant, but he also knew that Conchita would be totally loyal if he stoked her self-belief.

The door to the SIU main office crashed open. It swung violently back and thumped against the wall. The glass panel rattled. Ferran winced as he came in through the door waiting for the inevitable crash. It didn't come. The glass remained in tact.

'Phew. That was close. I must stop doing that……….. Gloria!' he shouted.

'Could you get that door fixed, the cushioning device doesn't seem to be working.' She looked up at him briefly from her computer screen and nodded. He headed over to Conchita who leapt out of her seat and was virtually dancing on the spot with anticipation.

'What's got into you Conchita?' Smiled Ferran as he approached Conchita, aware of her heightened state of excitement.

'I have some great news about this case Will. I searched the databases and found a few things but not a great deal. But then I managed to find a way into recently deleted files on the Mossos system. I don't really know how I got onto it but I found some interesting stuff.'

'Like what?' Ferran was now fascinated. He put his arms on Conchita's shoulders and gently forced her to sit down.

'Let's take our time over this Conchita, sit down. Do you want a coffee?'

'Yes please Will.'

He moved off to the small kitchen that was just across the room. There were no windows in the room, just a row of cabinets, a workbench, a microwave, sink, fridge and the very important coffee machine. There was coffee already brewed. He poured two coffees into two red mugs and walked back to Conchita. He placed the coffees on her desk and pulled up a chair on rollers right next to her. He looked tired but fired up. He was at last getting into this case. Conchita was bursting with information. She was desperate to tell him what she had found out.

'Go on then, tell me.' Smiled Ferran.

'Following your phone call earlier today with the information gathered by Esteban and Jesus, I got into the Mossos databases. I found the deleted files and one of them was relating to the death of the Englishwoman in Horta. Yes, it could just have been a file that was not wanted, misinformation, but it wasn't. It was a record of a call made by the Englishwoman to the police two days before her death asking them to come to her apartment, after she had been attacked.'

'By her husband,' quizzed Ferran.

'We don't know, as the Mossos obviously didn't respond to this call. It could have been because when they looked at her file they would have seen that her husband had apparently disappeared, although he had, in reality, turned up a week later.'

'It was probably just pure inefficiency or lazy detective work,' Ferran added. However, after her death they were probably embarrassed by this record and so got rid of it.'

Ferran was beaming. 'This is good stuff Conchita. Was there anything else?'

'Yes. This information spurred me on. The murdered woman's name was Sandra Peiron. Her husband was called Jose Reyes Lugano on the case sheet when she reported him missing. We have no record of this name anywhere. He doesn't exist.

But her husbands name is actually Jaume Felin Peiron.'
'Very interesting. Why did she give a false name? Did you search for other, similar situations?'
'Yes,' affirmed Conchita.
'What criteria did you use to narrow the search?'
'I looked for English women who were living in Barcelona and who had reported their husband or lover as missing.'
'Did you get any matches?' Ferran was getting interested.
Conchita smiled.
'Look.'
She pointed to her computer screen.
'There are three other situations, dating back to 1998, that match the criteria. There is no information whatsoever on the Spanish man Jose Reyes Lugano, although there is on Jaume Felin Peiron.'
'We need to check on insurance claims for the loss of life,' thought Ferran aloud.
'I'll get onto to that right away.'
'The husband of the Englishwoman is still alive, yes? But he was cleared of any involvement? Is there an insurance claim on his wife's life? He was in Madrid, apparently, when she was killed, but he could have been working with others.'
Ferran thought. His head rested on the knuckles of his right hand.
'Where does he live now?'
'Poble Nou.'

'Is he still an anaesthetist?'
'Yes, at the Hospital del Mar'.
Ferran left Conchita and poured himself another coffee. He had a lot to think about.

Chapter 32

Sandie Shaw, 'Like a puppet on a string'. The song by the nineteen-sixties British singer had haunted her all her life. Her parents were not to know, they were classical music buffs and had no link to popular culture. It had followed her throughout her life though. Boys at school would chant, 'Sing to us Sandie.' Later in life it was the song everyone wanted her to sing at the karaoke. For the first time in her life, she could see the funny side of this. She smiled to herself.

Her face soon returned to the frown it had been wearing for the past few hours as she thought of the beautiful detective Maria. She had unsettled her. Hadn't she given the police enough in her original interview? What more did they want? She hadn't liked the female detective. She found her pushy, but also she was too attractive. Women generally don't like it when they are confronted by intelligence and beauty combined in a superior package. Sandie Shaw certainly didn't like it. However, it wasn't as big an issue with her as it might have been. She rationalised things in her mind, which was a lot stronger now, and she told herself that she had done nothing wrong. This was the key to her new life. She was not going to live a lie. She was going to do what was right for her but she didn't want to live with regrets anymore. She hated being on the back foot and she had liked the strength of mind that she had developed recently. Sandie had made a significant decision over the past few days, from now on she was going to be truthful to herself and to others.

Her new lifestyle involved plenty of walking around the streets of Barcelona. She liked to get out and talk to people. It was quite amazing to her how much better her Spanish had become over recent days. She could even speak some Catalan now. Her change of attitude and situation had been very positive. She had started to engage with other people and she was pleased with the conversations she was having with Spaniards. Her favourite walk was a circular walk along the seafront, up the Rambla Poble Nou, onto the tram to Carrer Wellington and then back to Barceloneta. This walk and tram ride took her about four hours as she always stopped in a bar for a drink or a meal. She liked it more and more. She loved the Spanish way of life and the friendliness of the people. This was something she had not appreciated at all when she had been with Jaume. She knew, and admitted to herself, that her total infatuation with the man had limited her understanding and enjoyment of the real Barcelona. It had only been since his disappearance that she had really fully noticed and enjoyed the city. Originally Jaume had shown her the Ramblas and the other tourist hotspots. She loved them, but she now knew they were not the real Barcelona. She was now discovering what it was like to be alive in the real city. She was feeling strong, liberated and confident, probably for the first time in her life. Her love of the city was growing. Her money was running out, but already she was starting to formulate ideas for her future. She could easily run away back to Britain, but she was determined to stay in what she considered to be the most complete city in the world.

Chapter 33

Rambla Poble Nou is a much more realistic and naturalistic street than the tourist Ramblas. It is full of real Spanish people and virtually no tourists. The local Spanish parade up and down the Rambla or sit and talk on the benches or in the local bars. Sandie Shaw was strolling up the Rambla. She fancied a drink just as the rain started to fall. She found herself standing right outside a door to a bar. She braved it. It was bigger and lighter inside than she had considered and the atmosphere appeared friendly. She ordered a cerveza and got into a conversation in her pigeon Spanish with the barman. He started telling her about the change in the area over recent years. She could understand that he was remarking that there had been a great deal of new building in recent years, mainly apartments. These had replaced the old factories that had covered the local landscape for a long time. He felt the change was good. She agreed, saying that the area looked prosperous and exciting. A couple of drinks later, and she found herself ready to move on. The rain was still falling. Her head felt slightly light. Two beers mid-afternoon and she felt relaxed. She stood in the doorway of the bar waiting for the rain to ease.

She was in a very good mood. She had enjoyed the company of the barman. She hadn't thought about Jaume once today and she had slept well last night.

She felt good. Her gaze spread across the Rambla. She watched people hurrying through the rain. They either had their coats over their head or had umbrellas. The rain was now torrential. As she scanned the street her eyes locked onto a couple. There was a man, nearly six foot tall, slim and in his late thirties. He was dressed in black denim and his arm was around a woman in a red dress. She was extremely attractive and in her late twenties. He was holding his jacket over their heads and they were running towards the coast. She couldn't see their faces but she knew the man's body shape. She thought about it for a few seconds. By the time she had realised who it was they had disappeared out of sight. They were nowhere to be seen.

She stood rigid. She started shaking. The barman she had spent an hour or so in conversation with noticed her changed persona and he asked if she was OK. She pulled herself together and answered that she was. She left the bar and stepped out into the rain. The man she had seen was definitely someone she knew very well. She was convinced it was Jaume. There was not a doubt in her head. She was sure of it. Her mind had been playing tricks on her for the past few days, but she was now feeling strong and she hadn't thought of him for some time. She followed her instincts and rushed out through the torrential rain in the direction of the vanished couple. It didn't rain much in Barcelona, but when it did it was severe. She wore only a light dress and a cotton shawl over her shoulders. Within seconds her dress was clinging to her and her hair was lank. She ran down the Rambla Poble Nou. Her breasts were in their full form and in her wet dress they looked virtually naked. Any men she passed as she ran could not help themselves, their eyes just focussed on her large, round breasts. It was as if a wet T-shirt contestant had become stranded on the Rambla Poble Nou. She felt uncomfortable with men's eyes on her in this way but then in some ways she quite liked the attention. Their staring really didn't concern her though, not at this moment. She was thinking simply, 'Where did he go?'

Chapter 34

As she headed towards the coast along the Rambla Poble Nou she soon passed the main shops. She came to an area of open land on her left and apartments on her right. She stopped and looked around her. There were one or two people braving the rain but most faces that could be seen were in doorways or inside restaurants and bars. She moved around in a 360 degree circle. She was scanning carefully. In the distance along a side street she could see the couple she had spotted earlier. Through the downpour she saw them dart into an apartment building. She raced along the side street. When she reached the building they had entered she stood opposite and looked upwards, looking for a sign. Within a few minutes a light went on, then another. Someone had moved into an apartment. The windows of the apartment were not shuttered or curtained. It was a brand new block and had big, wide windows. In what must have been the kitchen window she could see the couple, they were kissing. As they parted the man was at the sink and he faced the window. Jaume stared down at her without seeing her. She was absolutely clear that this was her man. He wasn't a captive though. He had been abducted, hadn't he? Yes, it had been a set up but what was he doing running through the Rambla, laughing with that woman? How could he be here? She was very confused again. Her back was against the apartment block opposite the building she was watching. She was under cover and she slipped down the wall until she was sitting on the marble floor. What was going on? What was happening in her life? Her lover was with someone else.

Her sobbing was disconcerting and a number of men tentatively asked her if she was OK. She looked good, but she was distraught. Was she an attractive proposition or something to be avoided? The men who walked by her were not sure, but you could see the thought patterns going through their minds. She was stronger now though. She had released herself from the magic of Jaume over the past few days. She said to herself, 'Why are you crying? You expected this. Didn't you. Come on. Pull yourself together.' This she eventually did. She controlled her breathing and gradually raised herself to her feet. Her breathing was heavy and she was trying to control her thoughts. All of a sudden she felt very good. She realised that she wasn't that surprised by seeing Jaume, particularly, when she started to think rationally about it. Her acceptance of his actions hardened her. She did not like being wronged, but increasingly she didn't want him back.

The light to the main room in the apartment came on. She saw the woman in red in the room. She was too low down to see exactly what was going on in the fourth floor room. She turned and looked at the apartment ringers behind her. She pressed them all. Eventually someone clicked the lock. She pushed the apartment block door open and headed for the stairs. As she reached the fourth floor she pushed open the hallway window. Her view was unimpeded. She could see directly into the apartment opposite. It was a new apartment and there were no curtains yet. It was a big, expensive place with huge windows and a large balcony. By the time she got to her vantage point Jaume had joined the woman in the red dress in the main room of the apartment. Sandie could see everything. The apartment windows were floor to ceiling. The sofa was beige and there was a TV in the corner. The girl was fascinating. In her late twenties with black, long hair that was straight, probably straightened, Sandie thought. Her red dress was nowhere to be seen. She was dancing around the main room with only a pair of black, see-through panties. She had great breasts. Not too big but certainly not small and firm. She was hopping and skipping around the room. Sandie was amazed that she momentarily felt aroused by the sight of this lovely woman. She checked herself and saw Jaume at the back of the room. He was removing his clothes. She watched him become totally naked. His penis was always formidable but she had had to work hard to get it fully operational. She shuddered at the thought. He was big at his best and she had loved it. She looked across again. He was more than big and he was racing across the living area towards the woman. The two of them didn't care if anyone was watching. The passion was tangible twenty metres away. Sandie felt as if Jaume was coming for her. Then she realised and refocused. As he entered her from the rear the woman stretched erect before easing herself down to accommodate Jaume's passions. Sandie watched in disgust, fascination and growing anger.

She looked away in the end. As she began to realise that she was watching her lover, the man she wanted to marry, the man she shared ownership of an apartment with, the man she had left London for a new life in Spain for, the man for whom she had lied to the police. What was she doing? She slumped to the floor. The hallway she was in was very modern and very clean. Marble floors, white walls and very well lit. She rested for a while on the floor. Her thoughts were flying all over the place. She had learnt a great deal recently though. She had learnt a lot about herself and how to cope with setbacks. She impressed herself with how soon she assimilated what she had just seen. She stood up, walked down the stairs of the apartment block, hit the Rambla Poble Nou and headed for the coast. She was putting Jaume and what she had just seen behind her. Before long she was on the coastal promenade, walking back to Barceloneta.

Chapter 35

They were all in the SIU meeting room, the four detectives, researcher and administrator. The clock hands rested at one minute to six. There was silence in the room. Everyone was staring upwards at the large plastic clock on the wall. They waited. As the clock struck the hour they relaxed and Ferran spoke.
'OK. What a day! A very good first day for the SIU! We have moved a long way forward today. Jesus and Esteban, your work gave us the spark we needed, well done, and of course Conchita has again come up trumps with her research work.'
The three people mentioned by Ferran looked at each other and smiled, they were very self-satisfied. Ferran continued.
'Whatever we do, in every case, we must make sure we are thorough and find every scrap of evidence. I know I have a reputation for using my instinct, but what people often fail to realise is that my instinct is based on a foundation of facts. I am always thorough. You too, all of you, must always make sure that you look at every aspect of an investigation, from every angle and get the evidence.'
They all nodded, they knew they were in this team because they were good. They also knew that they were here to learn, to learn from one of the very best detectives. Esteban unbuttoned his top button. He looked exhausted. His youthful, clean-shaven

face was drawn and pale. Jesus just looked impassive. He rested as he listened. His body was almost shut down. Conchita, though, was still firing, her eyes were wild and she was alive. Ferran recognised their mood.

'Listen. I think we have done enough today.'

Esteban and Jesus visibly relaxed with a slump, whilst Conchita looked disappointed. Ferran caught her eyes.

'Conchita. You and I have work to do. The rest of you need to go home and enjoy the evening. We will meet again at 8 a.m.' Maria wasn't going anywhere without Ferran but the other three shuffled off into the night.

Maria, Conchita and Ferran prepared themselves for a couple of hours of further work. Maria got three coffees, Ferran popped out for some cheeses and chorizo. Conchita sorted her information. The three of them eventually settled down around the large wood topped table in the meeting room. The array of food and drinks were placed on the table. They were relaxed. Ferran and Maria looked like they needed a shower and a change of clothes. Conchita looked like she had just arrived, fresh, at the office.

'How are we going to move this forward?' asked Ferran.

'We know that ….no, actually, we know nothing,' he corrected himself.

'We think that the Englishwoman's lover, Jaume, is not really dead. Yes?' He looked at the other two. They nodded their agreement.

'We also think that he was not abducted and the alleged, observed murder was a set-up. Why?' Ferran paused.

'We also know that there was a very similar disappearance reported last year by the woman murdered in Horta,' checked in Conchita.

'The forensics might show that Jaume was involved in what appears to be a make-believe murder at the Palau Sant Jordi. It would be very interesting to match these findings with those from the Horta incident,' considered Maria. She leant back on her metal-framed chair. Her body shape was tired although her mind was still sharp.

'We need the forensics report. Without it we can do little,' said Ferran.

'You two have a break and enjoy your coffee. I'll go down to the forensics section on Gran Via.' The detective was already leaving the room as he spoke. Conchita and Maria were left alone looking a little bemused as Ferran disappeared out of the room.

Chapter 36

Ferran was enjoying this case after all. He wasn't sure which way his mind would go. Would he put his faith and belief in the Englishwoman and accept that she was actually telling the truth after all and that she had been set up in some way by this Jaume character? He didn't know. Or would he see her as a lying bitch, fully aware of what was happening and involved in the set-up? As he walked across the pavement along Via Laietana towards Gran Via his mind moved backwards and forwards, digesting and analysing the information he had. It was still light and the roads were busy. The shops were vibrant with customers and he found himself distracted. He realised this and walked more quickly, trying to avoid looking at what was going on around him. His mind was confused though. He needed to think a few things through. Just opposite at that moment, across the busy road was a small bar. It wasn't a tourist spot, and it looked fairly quiet and he needed a beer. Within a few minutes he was inside the bar, sitting on a stool drinking Estrella Damm.

The bar was nearly empty. He sat at the end of the long bar near the window. Seven or eight stools away from him sat a man. He was clean shaven and shaven headed. He was ageless and obviously a fixture of this particular bar. Behind the bar the barman kept himself busy by cleaning glasses.

Across the narrow room a young couple kissed over a table. Ferran sat and thought. He had to get into his mind the pattern of thought of the Englishwoman and Jaume. If they were working together what were they thinking? He sipped his beer. The thought processes started to engage with the case. Jaume had supposedly killed someone and then been abducted, but had she lied about it? If so, why? How could he be released by his abductors, there was no ransom note and, anyway, she had no money? What was it all for then? Why had she acted so convincingly? There had to be money involved, all this would be about money. He thought for a long time. His third beer arrived. He stared around him trying to think of a potential source of money.

The only possible solution he thought of was compensation or insurance money. But there would be no insurance money without a body and there was no body. He sipped his beer and surveyed the small dimly-lit bar. There was little happening and little to distract him. His brain was now more focussed. If it wasn't for insurance, then what was going on? If there was a link with Horta then maybe Jaume had done it before, maybe he was going to kill the Englishwoman and steal her money? But then, he thought, why would she play a part in his lies, unless she really did think she saw a murder and she really did think he was abducted? Yet his instincts had told him that she was lying, she had known more about what had happened to her at the Palau Sant Jordi than she had let on. There were too many questions still looking for answers. Two areas of thought would soon be resolved though. If forensics matched the items found at Palau Sant Jordi with those found at the Horta murder scene then he knew that Jaume had done this before. If they did match then the Englishwoman was possibly in danger. Also, he knew that if a body turned up in the next 48 hours purporting to be Jaume then they were going for the insurance money and the Englishwoman was involved. A body turning up three or four days after the incident would be sufficiently decomposed to hide many of the features and could easily be falsely identified.

He finished his beer and looked into the empty glass. He studied the remnants of foam that clung to the inside of the glass as a fortune-teller would study tea leaves in a cup, but he saw nothing that inspired him to chart an alternative course. He felt better though. He paid the barman and leapt, refreshed, back onto the busy street. Before long he was at the Mossos headquarters on Gran Via.

Chapter 37

Sleep just wouldn't come that night. She looked for it in every node of her brain but it avoided her grasp. As the minutes passed her mind felt more and more like a caged basketball. It rattled and bounced inside her skull. Painkillers didn't work. Nothing worked. She lay on her bed. It was a hot night. The air conditioner was on but wasn't powerful enough to make much of a difference, especially as she liked to sleep with the balcony windows open. It was comfortable lying on top of the summer duvet, but she couldn't sleep. She wasn't tired and she wasn't rested. Her mind was sharp, alive and in motion. Her thoughts were trying to escape from their prison, but they kept bouncing back. She couldn't rid her head of the image of Jaume. His buttocks clasped tight as he embraced the woman in red.

A little while ago she would have been in floods of tears by now, distraught. She had changed, over recent days. Changed for the better. Her head was full of thoughts, but they were of images and decisions she had to make, there were no emotions there at all. She felt in control and strong. It wasn't as if she had become a hardened man-hater as a result of Jaume. Her emotions were very much alive and in control. It was just that she was now free of Jaume's spell. Her thoughts kept wandering towards the detective she had not seen eye to eye with. She had forgotten his name and did not like him at all, but she had fancied him. She was thinking of men. The sight of Jaume and his lover had set her juices flowing and aroused the passion inside her. She crawled out of bed and walked naked over to the balcony. It was very dark outside. There was a gentle breeze blowing from the sea, it felt soothing on her skin. It was late and there was a lot of activity in the street below. As she glided past a chair near the open balcony she grabbed at a t-shirt lying across the backrest. She pulled it over her head and stepped out onto the balcony. For several minutes she stood resting against the ironwork of the balcony watching the people below. She found herself fascinated by the men. She smiled to herself.

As she watched the street below her thoughts returned to Jaume. What was she going to do? She had surprised herself that she didn't feel angry. She didn't want him back. She wouldn't have him back if he pleaded with her. She was totally over him as a lover and as a potential life partner. Her dreams had been wrecked but she wasn't unhappy about that. The fact was that he had got a share of her life, she was unhappy about that. Suddenly a look of horror spread over her face. She froze and gripped onto the iron balcony rail with her left hand. Her skin, in the dark lamp lit light, visibly paled. Why hadn't she realised before? What was she thinking? They had a joint bank account. There was probably €20,000 in it. Within seconds she was on her laptop computer logging onto her internet bank account. The statement appeared on the screen.

Life is a complete bitch sometimes. It is usually when you really don't expect it, but when it happens it knocks you sidewards. The computer screen glowed in the darkness and the white background framed perfectly the numbers that imprinted themselves onto her eyes. There was one withdrawal of €18,000, two days ago. All that was left in the account was €1,600. It was if the fight had gone out of her body. She fell off her chair and hit the tiled floor hard. She didn't care. There were no tears though. She just lay on the cool floor stunned. She wasn't dead, but a casual observer would have taken her to be. Her breathing was silent and she was motionless. Inside she was in turmoil. The money had been her security. It was everything she had. She ached with emptiness inside. It felt as if her intestines were collapsing and contorting. The longest twenty minutes of her life passed by as she lay motionless, waiting for her brain to finish rebooting.

As she came back into the world her thoughts were of concern for her safety. Survival was instinctive in her. She knew she had many faults but she was a real survivor. Her life was in danger, and she knew it. Jaume didn't care for her, he probably never had. Her stupidity was as annoying to her as her present clarity was startling. Jaume was after the insurance money on her life, that had to be what he was after, she thought. Her body realigned itself as she sat up on the floor. Her hands reached out for the frame of the chair and she pulled herself up to sit again in front of the screen. On her bank account she cancelled the monthly payment to their joint life assurance account and she e-mailed the life assurance company immediately cancelling the cover. She felt better instantly.

'He thinks he is sly and clever. He sees himself as a fox,' she said out loud. But inside she smiled to herself, as she knew she was much cleverer than him.

Chapter 38

A slight shudder ran through her body as she recalled that Jaume had, at the start of their time together in Barcelona, had another woman. She had all but forgotten about it, shelving the unpleasant fact in the recesses of her brain. He had given her up for him though, so she had forgiven him. Not this time though. He wasn't coming back into her life but she was not going to let him get away with a lot of her money, she wanted her money back. Her fear of him had subsided. She did feel though that he could kill, she had seen it in his eyes. The haunted glint that rested in the back of his eyes had always been fascinating to her. Perhaps it was because he had killed before. There was no way that he would kill her now the insurance was cancelled, there was no point.
'He doesn't know,' she said to herself aloud.
She paced around the room, her fingers pressed close to her mouth as she thought.
If he had intended to kill her how would he do it? The calmness of her mind whilst she was thinking these thoughts was surprising her. A realisation that it was actually quite exciting and enjoyable dawned on her. It was the middle of the night, it was sleeping time, yet she was a stimulated as she had ever been. How could this be? Wasn't her former lover trying to kill her? As the plastic chair on the balcony creaked from her weight being placed on it, she told herself not to be so silly. He

hadn't tried to kill her and he wouldn't yet. He was still trying to fool the police that he was dead so they could claim the insurance money. He couldn't know how she was feeling about him. To him she was still madly in love with him and was still reluctantly going along with the plan. Why then had he taken €18,000 out of their account? Did he not expect her to check the balance? She couldn't understand this. Maybe she was wrong. Perhaps he wasn't a killer. That haunted look in his eyes could be anything. Maybe he had used the money to pay someone to kill. He would need a body for the police to think that he had died. All these thoughts were new to her. They surprised her.

Thunder rattled across the dark sky, echoing around the narrow, apartment-lined streets. She looked up at the swirling towering clouds that were wrapped around the city. A storm was coming, she told herself. A smirk appeared on her face.
'A storm certainly is coming for you Jaume, my love.' The words crept from her lips threateningly. She had a plan. The rain hammered down from the violent sky. Within seconds she was in bed, fast asleep.

Chapter 39

The rain was hitting the ground so hard that it was bouncing back into the path of other raindrops, creating a strange surreal image of flowing water. The streetlamps rocked and swayed spraying light randomly, creating shadows that moved. There was no one about. Maria, Conchita and Ferran just made it to the door of the restaurant as the rains came.

'Oh, that was close,' squeaked Conchita.

They all stood inside the doorway and looked at the rain.

'Wow. That is a lot of water. Look at it. The drains can't cope,' remarked Ferran pointing to an overflow.

They were standing in the bar area that welcomed people into the Cuines Santa Catarina Restaurant along Avinguda de Francesc Cambó. They were hungry and so they bypassed the bar and waited at the entrance to the eating area. The place was, as usual, packed. They hoped there was a table free. The restaurant was huge and modern. It was part of the newly rebuilt Santa Catarina market. The market hall was behind the restaurant area but was built in the same modern style. The high, vaulted roof was under attack from the heavy rain and made a very loud noise. The feel of the restaurant was modern and chic. Ferran called to a waiter who was busily hurrying by and asked for a table. He signalled that he would be right back.

Before long they were sitting at a wooden table for four that nestled at the far end of the hall next to a climbing plant that gave their part of the restaurant a tropical feel. They were very near the cooking area that was open to view, with different chefs cooking the different types of meal the restaurant offered. Maria went for fish, Ferran pasta and Conchita meat. They had wine in their glasses and they settled down to talk whilst they waited for their food. They were still working.

'What did you find out from forensics?' asked Maria.

'Well, it was interesting,' replied Ferran as he shifted in his seat.

'There were a lot of prints from the flat at Horta. It looked as if it was a popular place. Or it is possible that the woman just had a lot of friends.' He sipped his glass of wine.

'So were the prints mostly male?' queried Conchita, looking very focussed.

'Yes, but they were quite old.'

'Quite old? What does that mean? How can they tell if fingerprints are old?' Maria was very tired and getting a little irritable.

Ferran looked at her. His eyes said softly to her, 'Calm down.' She took the message and cradled her drink.

'There was a print that matched the person we think of as being Jaume. That is if he was in the delivery area of Palau Sant Jordi. One set of fingerprints from the rubbish skips and from the oil bottle matched an old print at the apartment in Horta. Whether or not it was Jaume. The forensics team have no doubt that the same person was at the Palau Sant Jordi and at the apartment in Horta.'

'It could just be a coincidence,' considered Conchita intelligently.

'It could be a rubbish collector who lives in Horta and knew the Englishwoman.'

'It could be,' replied Ferran. 'Although I think it really could be our man.'

'What about the oldness of the prints,' chirped in Maria, still thinking along her earlier theme. She was less grumpy but had had enough. She looked very tired. Her eyes were red and bags were lying heavy below them.

'Baptista said that prints covered the building in Horta. They lay on top of each other. Our man's were less clear and partly covered by others. He felt that the prints of our man, Jaume, revealed that he wasn't there at her murder, unless he wore gloves.'

'Any DNA evidence?' Maria quizzed tiredly.

'Plenty from the Palau Sant Jordi but no match with Horta.'

Ferran sat back as the black shirted waiter arrived with three steaming plates of food. Ferran was impressed. How did waiters manage to carry so many plates? His mind returned to the conversation.

'So,' said Conchita with a mouth full of beef. 'We know that Jaume likes Englishwomen. There is his woman in Barceloneta and the dead one in Horta. There is a link.'

'Yes,' agreed Ferran. 'That's probably as much as we have got.'

Chapter 40

There was little else to say. Ferran looked in turn at his women. Even Conchita was looking tired and perplexed. He could see that she was delving deeply into her thoughts to find a link. Maria was spent. Ferran suddenly had a wake-up call. He switched in a nano-second from an ace detective, with the drive and desire to solve a troubling and important case, to a loving future husband with priorities that go no further than looking after his future wife. Maria was pale and struggling to eat her food.

'Maria. Are you OK?' he questioned. She looked dead tired and her eyelids were closed. Ferran leapt into action. He was a real action man when needed.

'See you tomorrow Conchita. Can you get home OK?' he added as an afterthought. She nodded. With that he stood up and lifted Maria into his arms. She was so light. He carried her across the floor of the restaurant and outside into the softening rain. He managed to hold her in his arms in a semi-conscious state, and flick his car lock switch open at the same time. He pulled the door open and lay Maria, his future wife, across the back seat.

Before long he had her relaxed in his bed at his apartment. She looked tired but he knew she was OK. He had undressed her sensitively and pulled the duvet gently over her body. Her face looked relaxed. She needed sleep. He didn't though. He felt really good. Interesting cases fired him up. He loved a challenge. He was firing on several cylinders. His apartment was huge. With Maria asleep in his bedroom he strolled down the apartment corridor in the centre of the building. He passed through the wood-lined walls of the corridor into the marble framed living room. The room was grand. Grey marble tiles covered the floor and white marble flooded the walls. The room looked fantastic and was enhanced by the minimalist furniture that sat around it. Ferran headed for his brown leather sofa. On the way he passed by the aluminium framed rosewood table that housed his drinks. He liked the occasional glass of Torres brandy. He poured one and sat on his sofa.

Ferran started tapping away on the keyboard of his MacBookPro laptop. He was halfway through his second book. He loved relaxing by writing. He wanted to be the next Montalban. Few people wrote crime thrillers set in Barcelona. He was to be the next great crime writer of Barcelona. His first book was OK in his mind and had sold several hundred copies. This one, though, was much tighter and far more exciting. When he got the chance he lived another life through his writing. Ferran had an idea for a central character that was not dissimilar to Harrison Ford, the actor. The character was a great detective known as Salvador Garcia. His current story featured an art theft. He sipped his brandy and headed off into the fantasy world of detective fiction.

Chapter 41

She had been sitting there since six a.m and had seen nothing. The bench she was sat on was hard and it was surprisingly cold. The coffee and pastry she had bought on the way were long gone and she wanted more. The sky was overcast and the sea was very calm, or at least it had been when she walked past it an hour ago. Her eyes were fixed on the apartment. Nothing. No movement, no lights and no action. It wasn't until nearly 9 a.m that a light came on in the apartment. She could see him. He looked tired. He made coffee and showered and dressed. Before long he was ready to come out of the apartment.

She watched him move to the door. She was waiting for him. The weather was ideal. Not too hot and not too cold. She didn't want to be seen. She was excited and alert. Her heart pounded but she controlled her thoughts. She sauntered over to the side of the road and stood behind a tree. Her position was some fifty metres from the apartment entrance. She watched. In a matter of seconds he came out. He looked both ways, but in the end he went towards Rambla Poble Nou at a brisk pace.

Ferran was crumpled in his seat. The white Seat Cortado was anonymous and he was invisible. Jaume walked right passed the car, he didn't see Ferran and Ferran didn't recognise him. As Sandie

Shaw came from behind the tree Ferran sat up in his seat. He was tired. It was four or five hours since he was curled up in bed. He had woken early and his instinct had told him to follow the Englishwoman. He always followed his instinct. His brain was dull from sitting there watching. Then the sudden movement of the woman aroused him although his body was not really prepared for action. He hadn't eaten that morning, which he scolded himself about. He told himself regularly that he was getting older and he had to take greater care of himself. Eat better and drink less alcohol. He took no notice of himself though. The black velvetine suit he had on was slightly crumpled from the several hours of stillness. His right hand brushed out some of the creases on his trousers. As the woman moved furtively along the street on the opposite side of the road to the car, she was rushing from tree to tree to provide herself with some visual protection, Ferran's eyes followed her carefully. He smiled to himself. He had a good eye for a woman and she wasn't unattractive. She was slim but a little heavy, had great breasts and an attractive face. Her clothes were her worst feature and lacked class.

Sandie Shaw disappeared around the corner of the road and out of sight. Ferran leapt into action. His body complained. His knees hurt, as they always did at this time of the morning. He put it down to the amount of football and basketball he had played until well into his thirties. He had been good, especially at football. He raced, despite his creaking bones, to the corner. He crept up close to the pink-rendered apartment building and peered around the corner. He was surprised to see her about a hundred metres away from him already. He crossed the road to get cover but he had to run to make up the ground. The sun was breaking through the grey clouds, burning them away. Ferran felt the warmth of the sun on him as he trotted along the road in pursuit of Sandie Shaw. The road was tree-lined and cars were parked on either side offering him plenty of protection. They were soon on the Rambla Poble Nou and there were people all over the place. Ferran just managed to keep her in his sights. Fortunately she was wearing a light green cardigan over a white linen dress, so she stood out from the crowd. By now he was within ten metres of her. He hated tracking people. He was tall and not good at keeping out of sight. It wasn't one of his strengths.

'Lo sieneto! Perdone,' he remarked quietly as he walked into an elderly lady, nearly knocking her off her feet. He helped her along carefully. Looking up he saw Sandie Shaw at the edge of the Ronda del Litoral, waiting at a crossing. He quickly edged up close to her. From behind a huge, middle-aged man who was straddling a bike, he could watch her unnoticed for a few seconds. She looked quite serene. She stood up straight and proud. Her stature was strong and she was composed in her actions. Through the crowd of people waiting to cross the road Ferran could sense that she was very focussed. She was looking at one thing and only one thing. The cars raced along the road. The lights took an age to change to red. Gradually the stream of vehicles came to a halt. Sandie Shaw was ahead of the other pedestrians as she sped after her target. Ferran had noticed her gaze. Her eyes were glued to a figure that had crossed the road earlier. By the time the lights changed the figure was only just in sight. He was tall, dark haired and in his thirties. Ferran had excellent eyesight and he tracked her prey as she closed in on him. He was strolling without a care. She was racing after him.

As they hit the seafront Ferran was only ten metres behind her. She wasn't aware of anything other than the person she was trailing. Ferran had had his eyes fixed onto the back of her head for the past twenty minutes and he hadn't seen her look anywhere except at her target. She was only a few metres away from the man she had been trailing. He, too, hadn't noticed anyone or anything untoward. He was smiling and ambling along, taking in the view of the sea and the cool morning breeze. There were many people about, enjoying the sea air along the promenade. He was dressed in a light tan jacket, brown shirt and jeans. He strode past the Baja Beach Club and headed off towards the Hospital Del Mar. In his wake Sandie Shaw and Ferran trailed. Ferran was intrigued. Who was this man she was trailing? He didn't recognise him. His brain worked hard, sifting the possibilities. In the end the only connection his mind could make was with the vague description he had read on the Mossos report of the alleged abduction. The man she was following looked vaguely like Jaume, her lover. Ferran tried to correlate the image with the reality. He wasn't sure.

Outside the main entrance the man disappeared into the hospital. Ferran watched Sandie Shaw and the man she was following. She didn't follow him. She stood for a second staring blankly at the glass entrance doors to the hospital as the opened and shut to let people in and out. Ferran decided to follow her prey. He rushed across the road and quickly walked alongside the hospital frontage and crept inside the doors. He hoped that Sandie Shaw wouldn't see him or recognise him.

Chapter 42

Inside the hospital people were streaming everywhere. It was a large, open entrance foyer with doorways disappearing off in every direction. He stood still just inside the door and raised himself on his tiptoes to make the most of his height. He quickly scanned all areas looking for him. On his third sweep of the hospital landscape he saw him. He was stood talking to another man, laughing and animated. Ferran wove through the throng of people between him and the man he was now following, as his target continued to talk. Ferran was in spitting distance of him when his conversation ended. As he moved off Ferran pounced. With a few strides he was standing directly in front of a very surprised man. He looked at Ferran initially with shock and then aggression.
'What is your game?' he said angrily.
'I would like to talk to you.' Ferran replied calmly.
'Who are you?'
'Detective Ferran of the Mossos,' Ferran said pointedly, flashing his detective card in front of his eyes. He had not yet got used to his new title of Chief Detective.
The man looked a little taken aback.
'What do you want?'
'Let's go down here. It's much quieter.' Ferran gestured towards a small corridor to his left that was free of people. The two men moved slowly into the area and stopped half way along it. They faced

each other. Ferran leant back casually against the cream, shiny smooth wall. He looked at the man standing opposite him. He was nervous and tense. This was a man with something to hide, thought Ferran. He also sensed that he was scared. He couldn't see this guy having the nerve to commit a serious crime. He was very attractive, and looked younger than he actually was. For someone in their early thirties he had few wrinkles and his features were very clear and well formed. Ferran used his experience to put the pressure on. He stood staring fiercely at the man for a few seconds. He wanted to see what he was made of. With his face reddening he gave the appearance of someone being basted with chillies under the skin. He was red and sweating. Ferran waited a little longer.

'Are you Jaume Felin Peiron?' questioned the detective.

The man looked even more concerned.

'Ye…Yes, that's me.'

Ferran decided to ease up the pressure. This guy was going to tell him everything he knew.

'Do you know a woman called Sandie Shaw, an Englishwoman?'

He broke down. He started sobbing. He put his arms around his head and cried. He slid down the wall and rested in a heap on the floor. Ferran hadn't expected this to happen. He stepped over to the man and pulled him to his feet by grabbing him under his armpits. The man stood easily back on his feet, pleased to get some support.

'Let's go and have a coffee. I need to speak to you.' Ferran's voice was slightly softer but still determined and directing. He was interested in what was happening. He sensed this man was basically a nice guy. His instinct told him so.

Chapter 43

Ferran still supported the man with his right arm under the left armpit as they reached the hospital café. Ferran sat him down on the nearest café chair and caught the eye of the waitress, signalling for two cafés con leche. He was a little tired after gently manhandling Jaume Peiron to the café. His large frame hit the chair.
'Let's start again,' he said gruffly.
'You are Jaume Felin Peiron. Yes?'
The man nodded. The tears had subsided although his face reflected their former presence.
'You know a woman called Sandie Shaw?'
The tears started to well up in his eyes again. Ferran though was having none of it this time. He grabbed Jaume's arm and gripped it tightly, forcing his eyes to meet his own. Ferran stared deep into them.
'You need to compose yourself, my friend and answer my questions.' Ferrans voice was rigid and it hit Jaume as if a steel bar had been rammed down his spine.
'Yes,' he whimpered.
'How do you know her?'
Jaume looked around him and spoke as he was looking at the waitress who was approaching them with their drinks.
'She was my wife.'
'Was your wife?' Ferran was confused.
'Yes, she was murdered several months ago.'

Ferran didn't understand this comment. He knew that Jaume's wife had been murdered but she wasn't called Sandie Shaw.
'Your wife was called Peiron, yes?'
'She was. But her name before we married was Shaw and I called her Sandy.'
Ferran had many questions.
'Why did she report you missing, almost a year ago, with a name of Jose Reyes Lugano?'
He smiled, remembering lovingly.
'She knew I would come back. I can't resist women. She knew it, but she didn't want me to get into trouble. She wanted me to know that she was concerned though.'
Ferran didn't understand this logic at all, but he moved on.
'Who were you with when you left?'
'Another Englishwoman, it was a real mistake but I felt a little responsible.'
'What do you mean?'
'I met this woman, Lydia Bart, in London when I went to train there last year. She fell in love with me. She was lonely and I was everything she had dreamt of. I couldn't get rid of her. I hoped that moving back to Barcelona would end the relationship.'
'Did it?'
'No. She sold everything up in London and moved to Barcelona. I met up with her and told her that I was married. She flipped. She threatened to kill herself if I didn't live with her.'

'So, what did you do?'
'I lived with her for a few days, but in the end I couldn't stand it.'
'Why?'
'All she would talk about was about us getting married.'
'What did you do then?'
'I couldn't take it. She was a nightmare, not my type at all. I told her I didn't love her and I left.'
'What happened then?'
'I haven't seen her since.' He paused. There was obviously more. Ferran pressed him.
'And?' Jaume looked at the detective and thought carefully before he spoke.
'After I left her she called me virtually non-stop on my mobile, fifty or more times a day. In the end I had to change my number. She followed me too. I used to work in the hospital at Horta, so I got transferred to avoid her.' Ferran was very interested in this.
'So it worked. Your change in job?'
'Yes, as I said. I haven't seen her since.'
Ferran reached into his pocket and took out a picture of Sandie Shaw, taken at the police station. He put it on the table in front of Jaume.
'Is this her?'
Jaume was shocked. She looked terrible. He hardly recognised her. But yes, it was her, Lydia Bart.
'Yes. It is Lydia.'
Ferran considered his words.

'You know she is calling herself Sandie Shaw and that she is following you?'
Jaume went white. The tears were long dried up.
'Keep her away from me please. I have a new life now. It took me a long time to get over my wife's death. One day I woke up and knew I had to make a new life for myself. I have met a most wonderful woman and I am happy.'
Ferran smiled at him. He believed everything he said.
'What do you do?'
'I'm an anaesthetist.'
'I take it that you were not at the Red Hot Chilli Peppers concert at the Palau Sant Jordi last week? Threw in Ferran almost as an afterthought.
'Yes I was. Why?'
Ferran was surprised by this answer. He considered whether it was worth asking his next question. He already knew the answer and it appeared ridiculous now.
'Were you abducted?'
For the first time since they had met Jaume smiled.
'No. Why?'
'Never mind,' Ferran replied slightly embarrassed.
'Listen. I will need to look into a number of things you have told me, but I can see no real reason to doubt what you have said. Take this card,' he passed a card with his contact details to Jaume.
'Call me if you need to tell me anything more. Could you write your contact details on this card for me?'

'No need. I have my own card.' He took one out of his wallet and handed it to Ferran.

'Now Detective, please excuse me. I have an eight hour shift in theatre and I am late. Can I go?' He looked enquiringly at Ferran. The detective leant back in his seat and stared at Jaume. He nodded nonchalantly.

Chapter 44

She looked at the hospital entrance in a trance. She stood with her back to the sea and stared. No one moved. Time was frozen. Everyone was still. Motionless. She stood up and walked amongst the still people. She went up to a young guy, a hip, young guy. She went right up to his face. He didn't move. She stared at him for a while. There was no noise, the seagulls were silent, the cars were stationary.

Her head pounded. It felt as if the Barcelona Metro was careering non-stop around her head. She was lying on her bed. It was really uncomfortable. Her mouth was dry and she could tell that her breath was impossible to live with. Slowly she raised herself. Her arms supported her as her body rose from the bed sheets. Slowly, as she lifted her brain from its safe harbour, she felt the pain. Her head really hurt. She managed to get out of the bed and raised herself onto her feet. Instantly the room moved. Not only the room, also the ceiling and the floor. They were spinning. She held her arms out straight, trying to find balance. Her breathing was regular but loud. Before long she was in control. Slowly she edged around the room to the kitchen. The sun was streaming through the windows of the apartment. She had no idea of the time. Her eyes searched for the big clock on the wall. Where was it? There. Ten minutes past three. It must be in the afternoon, her brain thought, it's still light.

She felt rough. The only thing she could think to do to remedy how she was feeling was to take a shower. The bathroom was wonderful in this apartment. It was fairly big, warm, well fitted and totally white. She climbed into the shower cubicle and turned on the tap. Water hit her head with a thud, cold initially but rapidly warming. The water was welcome and refreshing. Her eyes were shut at first and as she slowly opened them she saw the water was red. Why? Where was the red colour coming from? She searched the shower cubicle with her eyes. At first she thought it must be in the water but the water coming out of the nozzle was clear. Then she saw the source. There was blood on her arm. She must have cut herself. She couldn't think where.

Her mind was troubled. Where had she been all day? She couldn't remember anything about her day. She had no recollection about any part of it. She remembered having coffee in Pan y Mes on Passeig Joan de Borbon. After that, though, she could recall nothing. What was happening? Was it the drugs? She regretted the ecstasy and the LSD. Taking tabs and tablets had seemed like fun and an essential part of that fun. Originally there had been no danger, but as she clubbed more she realised that an evening out just wasn't the same without a tab or a tablet. She had known it was wrong and bad for her but she kept doing it. She was young, so what? It wasn't until she had a particularly bad trip that she tried to stop taking it. It didn't last long. She kept taking them. An LSD tab she had taken when she had first arrived in Barcelona had given her a really bad trip. She had found herself covered in blood and hyperventilating. Since then she had tried to get help, although she hadn't reduced her intake.

She felt better. It was sunny and warm outside. She went and stood on the balcony, looking over the newly rebuilt Barceloneta Market. As she looked out over the buildings and the open spaces she reflected on her life. She was very sad, she realised, although she was glad to have Jaume. He would be back with her soon and would normalise her life again. She was convinced that he would give meaning to her life. That was all she had wanted.

The lack of memory for the day bothered her. She went into the kitchen looking for food. She was surprised, there was hardly enough food for a mouse, yet she thought she had been shopping. Her memory bothered her and there was no food for her. The weather outside was atrocious. She felt no warmth and there was no one to support her.

Chapter 45

'Conchita!' roared Ferran as he returned to the SIU. Conchita was pleased to see him.
'I really don't know what is going on in this case. There is more to this but I just can't get my head around it.'
'What do you mean? What has happened?' asked an intrigued Conchita.
'I've found Jaume. The Jaume that this Englishwoman, Sandie Shaw, says was abducted.'
Conchita was excited.
'Where did you find him?'
'In the Hospital del Mar, but that is not important. The fact is, he was not abducted and he knows Sandie Shaw but that is not her real name, according to him.'
'What?' Conchita looked very confused.
'Her name is Lydia Bart. His wife, the woman murdered in Horta, or one of them, was called Sandy Shaw before she was married.'
Conchita lit up from head to toe, her batteries overcharged.
'You were wrong Detective Will Ferran, which I have to admit does not happen very often. But despite your initial reservations, this is a really interesting case,' she chortled.
'I am not totally sure about what exactly you are saying but I will get onto this woman's history. Let's see if there is anything about her. What can

we find? Let's see if we can find the truth.' She sat down at her computer and went to work.

'That's going to be useful Conchita, but the problem is, I really don't know what the truth is, or who is telling the truth. I need some time to think.'

Ferran went into the kitchen and poured coffee into a mug. He shouted out to Conchita to see if she wanted one. She didn't. He re-entered the office with a steaming hot coffee in his right hand. He sat at the computer opposite Conchita. Jesus and Esteban banged through the door at that moment. The door cracked against the wall.

'Hasn't Gloria got that door fixed yet?' snarled Ferran.

'They're coming tomorrow,' relayed Conchita.

Jesus and Esteban were looking pleased with themselves.

'What have you found out now?' questioned Ferran, sensing their confidence.

'We have found a link,' said Jesus. They both sat down in neighbouring seats and looked at Ferran and Conchita smugly.

'Well?' urged Ferran after a pause, looking for a response.

Jesus looked at Esteban, who used his eyes to signal for him to speak.

'We looked at the murders in Horta and tried to find any links between them. What we have found is that all four women were drug dependents. All of them had a real problem, mostly with soft drugs like cannabis, but they were all receiving treatment from the support unit at the Hospital del Mar.'

'The Hospital del Mar?' Ferran was suddenly interested. He had been there less than an hour ago.

'Yes. We checked and although they didn't attend clinics together there are a few individuals we need to investigate further. For example, there is a doctor working there who has previously been charged with supplying drugs. There are also a couple of other people we need to look into.'

'Do you have a list of all the out-patients?' asked Ferran.

'Yes.....somewhere,' chirped up Esteban as he rummaged in his briefcase.

'Here,' he said thrusting a piece of paper in front of Ferran. He quickly scanned the names. There were many people he knew. Some were friends. His eyes stopped at one name. Lydia Bart.

Chapter 46

Gloria bounced into the office. She had been in one of the outer offices working.

'You might want to hear this,' she said looking at Ferran. She passed him a recording on a mobile phone of a message she had just received from the Mossos.

'Body of a young woman reported dead in Poble Nou. The woman had been attacked severely with a sharp implement. Her name is Christina Reia La Portes. We are keen to apprehend her partner, Jaume Felin Peiron.'

Ferran leapt to his feet.

'That's him. I'm going back to the hospital. I know where he is.' The words trailed behind him in his wake as he dashed out of the office and headed for his car.

The sun was hot for the early evening and despite the lateness of summer there were a good number of people still on the beach. It was such an inspired place to locate a hospital, thought Ferran as he arrived outside the Hospital del Mar in his battered white Seat Cordoba. He really needed a new car and yet he quite liked the image the tatty Seat gave, busy and careless. He parked hurriedly outside the hospital, narrowly missing a bus just stopping to pick up its passengers. He moved with the elegance of a gazelle, he always did when he was focussed and in control. The hospital wasn't busy and the crowds that had filled the entrance foyer earlier in the day were absent. Ferran was hot and sweating but he knew what he was doing. He asked at reception for the theatres. He was directed and he took the lift. Ferran was amazed by how easy it was to get into and around the hospital as he peered into theatres and watched operations taking place. No one questioned him.

Chapter 47

He was looking for Jaume. The third operating theatre he looked in gave him some hope. It was hard to tell who was who in the theatre, especially as they were wearing green facemasks and smocks. The white ceramic walls and bright, clean lighting was quite surreal to someone like Ferran who spent his life amongst the grime and low life shit of the city. He was dazzled by it all, although his professionalism shone through. As he looked through a viewing window, at what looked like a cartilage operation on someone's knee, the anaesthetist looked back at him. Ferran saw recognition in his eyes. At that point the anaesthetist knew the detective needed to speak to him. Ferran watched as he tidied up the end of his part in the operation. It took ten minutes. Ferran didn't move. He didn't watch the operation, he watched Jaume Felin Peiron only.

The operation finally ended and Jaume made his apologies and rushed out to Ferran. He still had his surgical gear on.
'Detective. I am surprised to see you here again. You look agitated. What has happened?'
This annoyed Ferran. He wanted to look calm and in control. He had to play this carefully. Everything pointed towards this guy being guilty, but he wasn't sure. Everything pointed to his guilt, but it was seemingly all too obvious. He didn't want to

spook the guy either. Ferran took Jaume by the elbow and guided him along the corridor into a quiet alcove. He stood in front of him and looked him in the eyes. Jaume looked concerned.
'Your partner.'
'Oh no. Oh no, please don't tell me something has happened to her,' he cried out aloud. His eyes begged Ferran not to say the obvious. Ferran found it surprisingly difficult to get the words out of his mouth. His throat felt constricted and dry.
'Your partner, Christina Reia La Portes, has been found dead in the apartment you share.'
Jaume fell to his knees in silence. His eyes flooded with tears. Ferran helped him up and sat him on a nearby chair.
'I have to take you to the station to get a statement from you. We will, of course, fully investigate the incident.' As Ferran spoke the expression on his faced changed with the realisation that he wasn't just being informed of his lovers death.
'I didn't kill her,' he screamed.
'You think I killed her. You bastards thought I killed my wife too. I didn't kill her.....oh my beautiful Christina,' he wailed. Ferran gave him a few minutes and then decided it was time to move.
'Come on Jaume. We need to go.' They both stood up and, with Ferran interlocking his arm in Jaume's, they slowly walked along the well-lit corridor. Jaume wasn't saying anything and Ferran relaxed a little, confident that his 'witness' was compliant. It was late in the afternoon as they hit

the main hospital foyer. It was relatively quiet, although about thirty invalided people in their wheel chairs were entering the building from the street. Each had a helper and each was very slow moving. Ferran and Jaume stood to the side to let them through.

Chapter 48

In an instant he was gone. He caught Ferran off balance with a gentle nudge with his elbow. Ferran floundered on the shiny marble floor. Jaume zigzagged through the herd of wheelchairs and ran out onto the Passeig de Maritim. Ferran reacted quickly and was up on his feet in seconds. It was harder for him to get through the phalange of wheelchairs but he eventually made it. He had kept his eyes on Jaume, even as he had struggled to get back onto his feet. The large floor-to-ceiling hospital windows gave perfect visibility. He was some fifty yards behind him. Both were racing. Jaume was much younger than Ferran and could sprint. He immediately widened the gap. The detective wasn't fast but he was a good distance runner, always had been. He ran three or four times a week. It was good for his fitness and good for his health, that is what he told himself on the cold, winter evenings when he was pounding the streets in his running gear. He ran every other Barcelona marathon for fun too. He knew he could keep up with Jaume. After a few hundred yards Ferran was gaining on the tiring Jaume. They were heading across the small park that surrounded the old gasometer, a symbol of the industry that was the heart of the city fifty or so years ago. Ferran was gaining on him. Jaume reached the street at the far end of the park. He looked quickly back at Ferran. He saw that he looked strong. A group of youths were chatting at the roadside. Jaume then surprised Ferran. He pushed a youth off his scooter, quickly climbed on and headed off towards the Ronda Litoral.

The youths were angry and hurled stones after the departing Jaume. Ferran showed them his police badge and instructed the other youth with a scooter to lend it to him. He did so surprisingly willingly. He obviously wanted Ferran to get his man. Ferran climbed on the yellow scooter. He was enormous and looked really ungainly. He hated scooters. They were the scourges of the city's streets in his view, and now he was on one. He fiddled with the gears and tried to get something more than the twenty kilometres an hour he was currently getting. No good. He just putt-putted along. His heavy frame probably didn't help. He was going fast enough for his jacket tails to fly behind him in the airstream. Ferran could see Jaume on his red scooter not far ahead of him. He was obviously having real problems with his controls as Ferran was gaining on him. Ferran had him in his sights. He crouched his head down so it was just above the handlebars and looked determined. A group of elderly women just leaving a peluqueria caught sight of him coming their way. They laughed at the sight of this well-groomed, enormous man, tootling towards them on a tiny yellow scooter. Ferran couldn't resist the audience and saluted them as he went by.

Barcelona Betrayal

By the time he refocused on his target, Jaume had cut straight across the busy dual carriageway. Ferran had no choice but to do the same. He closed his eyes and headed across the busy road. A few cars nearly hit him but he reached the other side with a huge exhalation of relief. The red scooter had turned off towards the zoo around the Olympic Village Metro corner. This was a quiet open road. Few cars and few people. The same conditions existed along Carrer Wellington. Jaume headed straight along the tramlines before taking a left along the Ciuatadella Parc. Ferran guessed he was heading for the narrow, busy maze of streets of the Ciuatat Vella. He was right. Within minutes the two scooters were beeping their way through the throng of people along Carrer Flassaders. Jaume turned right at the end of the street. Ferran was thinking ahead. He turned right down a narrow alley before the end of the road. Jaume would go straight now, past the church of Santa Maria del Mar. This Ferran anticipated. He took a short cut. He came out right alongside Jaume who was so surprised he nearly fell off his scooter. People were scattering everywhere as the two scooters drove on side by side. Ferran was shouting to Jaume to stop, but he ignored him. They were just passing the memorial flame outside the church when Ferran dropped back slightly and turned his front wheel a little in order to clip the back of Jaume's scooter. The impact was instantaneous. Both bikes flew onto the brick courtyard around the eternal flame monument and both riders went skidding across the red bricks in different directions to their scooters. Ferran felt his leg. It was badly grazed. His velvet trousers were ripped apart and blood was streaming from his thigh. He got up quickly, under the circumstances, and jumped on Jaume. He wasn't going anywhere though. He had hit his head. He was OK, but groggy. Ferran was given some water by an onlooker and he threw it at Jaume's face. He came around a little. Ferran got him onto his feet. Together they staggered into a restaurant on the square called the Local Bar, to get Jaume out of the public gaze. Ferran kept an eye on him whilst they waited for the Mossos to arrive.

Chapter 49

He held the gun in his stronger hand. Five times he pulled the trigger and nothing happened. Was there a bullet in the sixth chamber? Charcuiter was sweating. His face was as wet as a baby's sponge. He sat, arms splayed wide, stuck rigid with fear in the office chair. In front of him was Jack Kavanagh, tall, strong and determined. Determined to rid the streets of Barcelona of filth like Charcuiter.
'I didn't do it....it..it wasn't me. Would I tell you a lie, Jack?'
'Don't waste your breath, you scum. This world has seen enough of you and your slime. Goodbye.'
The trigger clicked. The gun fired. At the last split second Jack Kavanagh used all the gun skills he had mastered during his ten years with the Spanish Foreign Legion in Morocco and gently altered the trajectory. Charcuiter gasped as the gun fired. His eyes were closed. Then nothing but the sound of laughter. He opened his eyes. Jack Kavanagh, 'detective extraordinaire' was smiling.
'Did you really think I would let you get away with it that easily? I think a spell in prison amongst some of your former friends and allies will be a far more appropriate course of action.'
He laughed again.

Where was this story going? This was the second Jack Kavanagh thriller he had written. The first

had sold a few hundred, so he was pleased he had a following, although he would love to be thought of alongside the great Montalban. Ferran paused in thought at his computer screen. He was sitting at the dining table, looking at his laptop. His leg hurt and he winced when he moved. Writing his latest thriller took his mind off everything. It was seven in the evening, Ferran had been at home for an hour or so. His leg had been repaired and Jaume was in the cells, pending further investigation. He was relaxing, enjoying his second love, writing detective fiction.
'Hola, my love,' breezed in Maria, now his first love, resplendent in gorgeous green from head to toe.
'What is that on your head?' queried a mystified Ferran.
'It's the latest Lagerfield creation. Don't you like it?'
Ferran avoided the question in the hope that his future wife would take the hat off and consign it to the wardrobe that they were destined to share.
'I spoke to Kay today. I told her our news. She was delighted. We will invite them won't we?' she stated as she carefully removed the offending item from her head and placed it on a table.
'Oh yes. I love Kay. She is beautiful,' he thought for a second and considered what exactly Maria was talking about.
'Invite them to what?'
'Our wedding of course!'

'When? I don't remember fixing a date or anything,' stumbled Ferran in a mild panic.

'Don't worry Will. We haven't done anything yet. But, I think we should plan it all this weekend. Yes?'

Maria had his face in her hands and was planting her delightful lips on his. She smelt like heaven must smell on a good day. Her skin felt as soft as a peach and she looked divine. What could he say?

'OK.'

Chapter 50

It was eight thirty or later in the evening. Ferran and Maria were early. Bar Jai-ca in Barceloneta was bursting with positive atmosphere. The bar was definitely a Barça F.C place. The picture on the wall was of the great Kubala, the hero of the 1950s. They sat on a couple of bar stools, eating piemientos and sardines. Before long Charlie and Kay Lowson, an English couple, who lived in Barceloneta and had teamed up with Ferran and Maria on a case last year, arrived. Shortly afterwards their mutual friend Roma Bosch, a Catalan lawyer and Barça F.C fanatic, joined them in the packed bar. Tonight it was Chelsea v Barcelona in the Champions League. Bar Jai-ca was as good a place as any to watch the game.

The bar was on a corner of two streets. It opened onto the road outside and in the summer had a few tables out there. Today, in late August, it was inside comforts only. There wasn't a space free in the bar. Every seat and every vertical space was taken. It was quite a small TV that held everyone's attention, but it was the atmosphere that attracted them. The place was alive. The bar staff were busy, either serving drinks, a range of tapas or remonstrating and laughing with the clientele.

The five of them had a great night. Barcelona won, away from home. They were, all three, very pleased for Ferran and Maria on hearing their news and Roma informed them all that he had just been made a senior partner in the law company he worked for. The drinks went down rapidly followed by only a small amount of food. At eleven thirty p.m all five were staggering along the road until they hit Passeig Joan de Borbon. They stopped and regrouped.

'Where did we leave the car Maria?' asked Ferran in a voice highly influenced in its tone by a great deal of alcohol.

'We came by Metro, Will,' she replied with some exasperation.

'The Metro is still running, but it will take you half an hour to get home. Just look at you two, you are exhausted. Stay with us tonight. There is room. You too Roma,' offered Kay.

'No. I am OK. I have an important meeting at 8 a.m in the morning I need to get home. Adios. I will be in touch.' With that, Roma was gone.

'What about you two?' asked Charlie. Just as he spoke Ferran decided to sit on the pavement. He felt tired. Maria agreed that the Lowson's apartment, two roads away, was the best bet. Charlie helped Ferran to his feet and they headed home.

Chapter 51

'Throw me a line I'm sinking fast.' The first line of the Roxy Music/Bryan Ferry hit, Virginia Plain, rang out from a mobile phone resting on the radiator. He didn't move. A hand reached across his sleeping body and picked up the phone. Maria answered the call.
'Hola, Maria.'
'Hola Maria. Gloria here at the SIU. Are you both coming in soon?'
'In about an hour I would say. We had a good night last night,' she laughed.
'I'm pleased. You two are so good together. Were you planning your wedding?'
'No, that is for this weekend,' confided Maria.
'Where are you?' asked Gloria.
'In Barceloneta.'
'Bueno. I need you to pick up the Englishwoman, Sandie Shaw.'
'Why?'
'A body has been found in the harbour, they think it is Jaume Felin Peiron. Documents were found on him.'
'What?' Her face flattened out with surprise and she sat back in the bed.
'I don't understand how that could be. He was picked up by Will last night. He's in the cells at Gran Via,' she replied incredulously.
'Yes I know, but they have this body and they found cards and papers on it that say it is him,' continued

Gloria, exasperated as if she had had this same conversation several times already.

'The body is in the morgue in the Raval.'

'OK, we'll pick her up.'

It took Maria quite some time to rouse Ferran. He had drunk a great deal of water the night before, fortunately, and, as a result, he was relatively sober when he awoke. A shower later and Maria, Charlie and Kay joined Ferran heading down Calle Sant Miguel. Within minutes they were sitting on the stools around the three-sided bar of the New Orleans Tea and Coffee Company café on the edge of the Barceloneta market. It was the favourite café of them all. Basic and busy, the coffee and chocolate croissants were great. The waitresses each had a side of the bar to manage and they were in perpetual motion. Making, cleaning and serving. Great coffee, great service and a taste of the real atmosphere of working Barcelona. Ferran just sat and enjoyed the vibes. He had travelled quite extensively, covering a large section of Europe and had spent a week in San Francisco and two weeks in Buenos Aires. He had liked the Argentinian city, but it was no match for Barcelona, no city matched his city. Barcelona was the complete city. Why go anywhere else? Kay and Charlie Lowson were English but shared Ferran's sympathies. They had travelled a great deal, but for people like them who liked culture, activity and a city with an 'edge', Barcelona was unbeatable. It was hard to describe the city to someone who had not experienced anything outside the Ramblas, but they didn't care. If, after a visit to the city, you didn't love the place, then you were probably immune to the magical essence of Barcelona. After an hour of good coffee and company Maria and Ferran said 'adios' to the English couple and headed over the road to the building that housed the apartment of Sandie Shaw.

Chapter 52

As Maria pressed the silver button, the bell to the apartment rang. The two detectives looked OK, despite wearing the same clothes they had stood in the night before. They waited. After a few minutes a voice came over the intercom.
'Who is it?'
'Detectives Tupelo and Ferran.'
'Uh.'
Nothing happened. The detectives waited for a few minutes. Then they heard someone coming down the stairs in the apartment stairwell. The metal door to the apartment block was very ornate and Ferran remarked that it reminded him of the Casa Miro. Maria never found out why. Ferran was just about to explain his thoughts to her when the apartment door opened and out stepped Sandie Shaw. She saw Ferran first and her look of complete disdain was evident. She then focussed on Maria and the hardness of her facial expression marginally softened. She stepped onto the pavement and stood alongside the two detectives. Nobody said anything. Looks were exchanged. Maria broke the ice.
'A body has been found. We need you to identify it.'
She looked bad. Her skin, despite a tan, was grey and tired. She looked like a beautician after two weeks in a Soviet labour camp. Her manner suggested that she hadn't heard what was said to

her. She was staring at Maria blankly, but the words didn't register.

'Sandie Shaw? Did you hear me?'

The two detectives glanced at each other. Sandie Shaw stumbled as she refocused, this time on Ferran. She was either completely stoned or, as they both felt instinctively, she was mentally unstable. Her actions were awkward and unusual. Her mind was on another planet. She wasn't seeing or hearing anything. Ferran touched her on her right elbow and she swung dramatically around to face him. He reeled away from her with a quick step backwards. She focussed on him.

'OK, where do we go?' she asked in surprisingly friendly voice. Ferran was not impressed though.

'Get in the car,' instructed Ferran. He walked across the pavement, held the door open and forced her, through his powerful bodily presence without feeling or care for her, to get into his car. Maria followed.

The beat-up Seat bumped into the curb at the morgue in Raval. The three passengers forced themselves out of the car and walked towards the brand new part of a very old building that housed the dead body. The electronic, automated doors were at odds with the nature and purpose of the building. They were modern, fast and efficient. Within seconds they were inside. Ferran fixed the location of the body and explained the purpose of their visit with the mortician. The room they stood in was surprisingly small, low-ceilinged, with white fluorescent tubes that reflected dead light. The room smelt like clean, sanitised death.

A dead hulk, purporting to be Jaume Felin Peiron was soon wheeled in front of them. The tray had been pulled out of the freezer and the white sheet that covered the unfortunate shell of a body was removed by the mortician. Sandie gasped as she saw the face of the dead body. From their expressions of sympathy, it looked as if Ferran and Maria felt for her because they presumed she hadn't seen many dead bodies. Yet in reality it wasn't that. She had gasped because she recognised the body.

'Is this Jaume Felin Peiron?' asked Maria.

Sandie Shaw could not speak. She stared at the dead body. The pale, grey skin that wrapped the body made it appear translucent. She couldn't see a body in front of her. She saw a celestial being. She stepped back against the wall. Her eyes showed her inner fear. Slowly, as she analysed the dead hulk, she calmed down a little. The dead body that lay in front of her was the body of the tramp she had seen in the Parc Estacio de Nord, a couple of days ago. His eyes stared at her. She could still hear his words ringing in her brain, 'You are selling your soul'.

'It's not him.' She was definite. They knew it wasn't Jaume but he did have a wallet with his name in.

'Are you sure?' Maria quizzed steely.

'He had identification on him. His wallet says it is Jaume,' Maria stated firmly.

'Maybe he stole it,' suggested Sandie.

Ferran knew otherwise. He had suggested to his team that if Jaume was looking to claim insurance money, then a body would turn up dead within a few days. Ferran was convinced they had got their man. He looked at the sad, confused woman. For the first time he felt sorry for her. The woman in front of him was just a pawn in Jaume's game. She looked distraught and spent in every respect. She looked ageless, but that wasn't good. It was just impossible to tell if she was young or old. He couldn't understand why she hadn't lied to support Jaume's plan. Surely she was expected to confirm his identity? If she had, it would have given him the proof of death he needed for his insurance claim.

Maria came over towards Ferran and they discussed their next move. Sandie Shaw was standing, shrinking into herself, against the wall. She was staring at the floor.

'I need to get back to Gran Via and find out what Jesus and Esteban have got out of Jaume,' Ferran asserted. He looked good now. His body had started to function normally. His black hair was just right. He had discovered a new conditioner, 'Gliss', that he applied every single day. He wasn't vain, but at his age he had decided he needed all the help he could get to hold back the years. He liked the way his hair felt soft. He felt good.

'OK. Do you want me to take her home? Do we need anything else from her?' asked Maria.

'No, I don't think so. Just make sure she is OK, she looks as if she might do something rash. I'll take the Metro.' Ferran tossed the Seat's keys to Maria and headed for the door.

'See you later.' He waved.

Chapter 54

The Raval was alive with people as Ferran wandered towards the Ramblas. This was his least favourite part of the city, mainly as it was full of too many bad memories for him. The cityscape was being rapidly developed and it wasn't anything like the decrepit and dangerous Raval of his youth. His early years as a policeman were spent here amongst the prostitutes, pimps, contrabandists and dealers. It had been a dangerous introduction to police life, although on reflection he appreciated it had also been good for him. The dangers the area presented had made him determined to get fit and to learn how to defend himself. Despite a lot of dedication and hard work in developing his self-defence skills he didn't come out of his spell in the Raval unscathed. Once, whilst arresting a beautiful blonde prostitute, a pimp had slashed his stomach with a knife. An inch higher and the result could have been very different. Then a few months later, during a routine patrol, he and a colleague were set upon by a gang and badly beaten. As with any harsh experience he had been given an important lesson. He had learnt to be so much more aware of his intuition and he discovered the skill of taking evasive or offensive action well before an incident had even happened.

The Raval redevelopment was good and was making a significant improvement to the quality of life of the people in the zone. He didn't like it though. He missed the stench and the decay. It was a little piece of Barcelona that he wasn't proud of but he still liked. Before long he hit the Ramblas. This road was beautiful, but only early in the morning or when it was cold and rainy these days. The crowds of tourists were relentless. Ferran liked it though. He loved the noise and the people. He walked along enjoying the sight of the tree tops, which were the only part of the Ramblas he could clearly see. Liceu Metro station was in front of him. He hurried down the set of stairs and bought a ticket. The train was there within seconds and he soon found himself standing at the top of the exit of the station at Plaça de Catalunya. He was thinking about what to do. The Mossos headquarters on Gran Via was not his favourite place. He stood to the side of the pavement to get out of the way of the streams of people making use of the Metro. He called up Esteban. He and Jesus were at Gran Via. Ferran arranged to meet them at the SIU on Via Laietana in thirty minutes.

Chapter 55

The SIU offices were roasting. They were so hot that Conchita was sitting at her desk in only her camisole and a pair of shorts. All the windows were open. Gloria was berating a couple of workmen who were trying to fix the boiler, which was the cause of the high temperature. Ferran took off his jacket and loosened a few buttons on his shirt. The three detectives, Ferran, Jesus and Esteban sat at the table in the meeting room as close to the open window as possible.
'Let's run through what you two have found out then,' stated Ferran. He was feeling that this case was nearly sorted in his mind, although he just wasn't sure. His instincts were telling him that they were heading in the wrong direction.
'What has Jaume told you?'
'Well,' jumped in Esteban. He was still looking pale. This was developing into quite a big case. For a young detective, being given such a big role was very tiring. His body looked exhausted, yet his eyes were still keen. Ferran made a mental note to help Esteban develop his stamina. This was a tough job, with awkward hours that weakened your body, yet there were certain actions you could take to limit the damage. Esteban would be worth the time and effort he considered.
'He denies everything. He said he was at work, in the operating theatre all day. He only left for thirty minutes to get lunch from the canteen. We have

checked that he was at work when he says and we are now looking at the hospital CCTV to check if he did just stay in the canteen at lunchtime.'

'What do you think?' asked Ferran. Esteban looked at his partner, Jesus.

'We have talked a great deal about this Detective Ferran. We expect the CCTV to show that he is telling us the truth. There is little possibility that he left the operating theatre. The senior surgeons he worked with all say he was there for the whole time. We believe that if he killed Christina Reia La Portes, then he must have done it first thing in the morning,' Jesus reported.

'We asked him about the death of his first wife and he was in Madrid as reported at the time,' continued Esteban.

'He could have paid people to do it on both occasions,' interjected a thoughtful Ferran.

'Yes, but why? There was no life insurance on Christina. We checked. Everyone we have spoken to so far has told us how much in love Jaume was with Christina. Why kill her?' Esteban was obviously troubled by this case.

'An argument?' Ferran offered.

'Possible. He does seem the obvious killer, but we found out more interesting information,' said Jesus.

'You two have done well,' commented an interested Ferran. He rearranged his clothes as he was sweating profusely, his trousers sticking to his skin. 'Tell me,' he instructed.

'You remember that Conchita found a link between all the women killed. They were all drug dependents attending a clinic at the hospital. That Englishwoman, Sandie Shaw, was linked too. Well, we looked into this. Two of the people operating the clinic, a doctor and a male psychological nurse, were supplying the names of their patients to a couple of local drug dealers, in return for their own free supply,' Esteban relayed.

'How do you know?' quizzed Ferran.

'They told us.'

'Just like that?'

'Jesus may look gentle,' smiled Esteban wickedly, 'but he is very forceful when he has to be.'

'They told us the names of the drug dealers. Also, when we picked them up, we found that they were real amateurs, totally out of their depth, but the scary thing was that two Mossos detectives were protecting them. That is why the murders of the women have not really been solved. Everything has been hidden away and buried. It appears as if the detectives were getting the names from the two characters at the hospital and then feeding them to these two drug dealers,' finished Jesus.

'In return for a percentage of the profits. They were protecting the dealers and their income, that's why the murders have been hushed up,' added Esteban. 'The detectives controlled the whole operation.'

'I reckon Jefe Perez knew that. That must be the reason he gave us the case. No one else would have got inside it,' thought Ferran out aloud.

'Why do you say that?' questioned Jesus, looking puzzled.

'You will learn quickly about the Mossos, Jesus. You will have to decide if you wish to join in with the corruption, which is endemic, or go your own way, which is lonely and painful. Jefe Perez knows that none of us are corrupt and we would look fairly into the case.'

'We still have some further work to do on this Ferran.'

'I can see that, but do you have the hard evidence to support your conclusions?' asked Ferran, really agitated and excited by the news the young detectives had given him.

'Yes, it is all on tape,' replied Jesus.

'Who are the detectives?' Ferran wanted to get the bastards. He was extremely pleased with his two young detectives.

'Caballero and Sanchez,' presented Esteban.

Ferran nodded to himself, knowingly.

'You two have done well. Now we need lunch. Tell me a place you like to eat near here?'

'There's a fairly new place down Princesa, it's called Txirimiri, it serves tapas and meals and the house red is good. Not too expensive either,' suggested Jesus.

'OK. Let's get out of this sauna. First, we need to tell Jefe Perez Camps about what we know. Are you both OK with that?'

Esteban and Jesus both nodded.

Ferran spent some time on his mobile to the Jefe. He was quite animated in his conversation. Eventually he relaxed and it became quickly obvious to the young detectives that the Jefe was on his way to join them for lunch.

Chapter 56

She was captivated by the dead body. It lay on the stainless steel trolley, part covered by the white sheet and immobile. The body looked surreal, positioned as it was without a frame, the whiteness of the walls and floor creating a seemingly edgeless landscape. The face of the old man haunted her. The words he had said to her in the park continued to torment her mind.
'You are selling your soul.'
She tried to work out what he meant. It bothered her that deep inside her mind there was another vision of him. She had seen him somewhere else. Where was it? Why did he have Jaume's wallet on him? Why did he single her out to speak to her in the park? She thought and thought again, but it was no good. She had no answers. Her mind was whirring like a stuck floppy drive. Her thoughts jumped around but the same ones kept coming back again and again.

Maria was standing at the back of the white room. Ferran had gone, probably thirty minutes ago. Sandie Shaw had looked like she needed some time to get her thoughts together. Maria decided to leave her to herself for a while. She looked as if she was somewhere else. Her body appeared vacated and devoid of life. She stood dead still, staring at the dead body. As Maria stared at her she noticed the vibrancy held captive in her body. She was still but her veins were running hot. Maria could see them standing out and the artery in her neck pulsating violently. All this was in discord with her serene expression. To Maria it was if her mind and body were separate entities.

The green and mustard checked outfit that Maria was wearing looked really expensive, although it was actually from Mango – expensive but not prohibitive. However, whatever she wore she looked classy. She should really have been a model she was so perfectly formed. She didn't want to have children and there is no doubt that children would have ruined her near-perfect figure. Maria was always aware of how she looked. She noticed other women and she noticed Sandie Shaw. She wore a smock. It was like something out of the seventies. Purple tie-dye and cheesecloth. She looked crap, completely crap. Maria was seven or eight years her senior but at that moment she looked much the younger.

Her gaze had moved from the old, dead man. She was intent on resolving the issue of freedom in her mind. The challenge was to control theses random thoughts and images. At least she was now aware of what was running through her brain. She had to find another focus, somewhere else to take her mind. Her eyes rested on Maria. The detective was looking at a message received on her mobile. She started to text a reply. Sandie Shaw was fascinated by the slimness of Maria's fingers. They were slender and tanned, with flashes of gold jewellery expertly placed to enhance the image. Her skin was smooth and delicate, with very little fat between the skin and the bone. She could see not only a slim figure beneath the trouser suit, but a highly toned figure. Maria looked fit and strong but not muscular. She wondered how much work it took to get a figure like that. She tried to look inside Maria's mind. She wondered what her life was like and if she had a man. This thought took her back to Jaume. She was looking forward to having him back, having him hold her in his arms again. She couldn't remember the last time they were together.

Chapter 57

Maria looked up. She sensed that Sandie was getting her head together. She watched her for a minute before speaking.
'Would you like to get a coffee before I drop you off at home?'
Maria felt little sympathy for the woman. She didn't like her and she didn't get good vibes from her, but she wanted to understand her more. She particularly wanted to find out why she had made up, or so it appeared, the story about the abduction. Sandie Shaw looked back at her. Maria could see her mind trying to engage with the words. Slowly she replied.
'Yes……..Yes …that would be nice.'
They walked out of the mortuary and were soon into the street under the midday sun that was just completing its rout of the early morning haze. The sky was nearly completely lucid blue.
'It's warm enough to sit outside. How about that terrace over there?' Pointed Maria. It was warm and an avenue of silver barked trees framed a lovely tranquil Barcelona image. The café terrace was by the side of a quiet road and was bathed in sunshine. The aluminium tables and chairs were decorated with red tablecloths and red seat cushions and, of the six or seven tables there were only a couple free. Sandie Shaw said nothing but just followed Maria's lead and sat at a table.

Barcelona Betrayal

The two women sat silently at the table. The waitress came and they both ordered a café cortado. Maria was keen to discover something about her coffee-mate.

'How long have you been in Barcelona?' she asked.

Sandie Shaw was surprisingly alert, and she answered immediately.

'Six or seven months now. It feels like longer. Jaume has made me feel very at home here. Where are you from? Are you from this city?'

Maria was surprised with the sharpness of the reply.

'No. I'm from Tarragona, just south of here,' she replied giving away more information than she had wanted.

They both sipped their steaming coffees. Neither looked at each other. Maria tried again to open up the conversation.

'What are you and Jaume going to do when you get back together?'

Sandie Shaw looked like thunder.

'What do you mean get back together? We are together. He loves me and I love him. We met in London about a year ago. He told me then that he loved me like he had loved no other woman and that is no different today.'

Maria saw her eyes glaze over as she spoke. It was like a rehearsed speech. She didn't appear to believe it but it was in her psyche.

'Where is he now?' Maria delved, trying to catch her off guard.

'I really don't know. Perhaps he's working. He spends a lot of time in other countries either training or training others.'
Maria was aware of her lies. It was hard not to be. Everything Sandie Shaw was saying was quite unbelievable. Maria knew it was pointless trying to engage her much further. She looked unstable and her words were unreliable.

After several minutes of silence, Maria suggested to Sandie Shaw that they left the café. Sandie Shaw nodded. They moved off and eventually got into Ferran's battered white Seat. The two women sat in silence as Maria fastened her seat belt. She noticed that Sandie Shaw didn't bother with hers. Maria didn't care. She started the car and slowly escaped the Raval.

Chapter 58

Txirimiri was quite busy, but not too busy to prevent the three detectives from claiming a prime table, located right in the centre of the window. Plenty of room and light. This place was a wonderful find. Ferran hadn't been here before but he was enthralled. The long bar to the side of the restaurant served tapas and beers and the rest of the high-ceilinged room was set out with tables and chairs. The building had been roughly prepared. The original brickwork exposed to create a rustic feel. Ferran loved it. It was a Basque restaurant and prided itself on serving original Basque recipes. They ordered a collection of tapas to share, including a great order of spinach with raisins and a variety of seafood.

This had the makings of a good team, Ferran thought to himself. Esteban and Jesus were young and inexperienced, but they had plenty of balls and intellect. Most importantly they used their initiative and made things happen. He liked them and they seemed to like him. As they chatted about the qualities of Txirimiri their food arrived, exactly at the same moment that Jefe Perez Camps strode in to the restaurant from the street.

'Hola!' The bull of a man bellowed across the room. He was, as usual, impeccably dressed. He powered his way over to the table and landed on a chair.

'Good to see you Jefe,' greeted Ferran. Esteban and Jesus quietly said their welcomes. Neither had ever met the Chief before and were slightly in awe.

'How do you always look so good? Do you dress yourself or have you a personal assistant who chooses your clothes and looks after you?' laughed Ferran admiringly.

'Hah. You can talk. How do you look so cool even in scruffy clothes, Ferran?'

'Scruffy clothes?' Ferran looked indignant and mock hurt filled his eyes.

'There is nothing wrong with taking a little pride in your appearance. A tidy body leads to a well-ordered mind,' Jefe Perez Camps chortled.

'Anyway, it is my lovely wife who has the tidy mind and the eye for fashion. She insists that I dress well and who am I to question the Generalissimo?'

The two young detectives relaxed marginally as the two more senior policemen joked.

'Would you like some food Jefe?' asked Jesus.

Jefe Perez Camps looked at him, startled at the new voice.

'No. Thank you. But don't let me stop you eating. I have already eaten. I will share your bottle of wine though. Is that OK?'

Jesus signalled OK with a nod. Jefe Perez Camps signalled to a waitress for an extra glass.

The food was good and was quickly devoured. Jefe Perez Camps kept them up to date with the latest and most interesting cases whilst they ate. Eventually they were all ready to talk in detail.

'Ferran tells me that you boys have done some extremely good work. Your findings implicate some of our detectives I understand. Could you tell me exactly what you have found and show me the evidence?'

Ferran looked at the two young detectives. He could see that they were a little apprehensive about speaking ill of fellow detectives with such a senior officer. They were young and a little naïve, but already they knew that corruption hit the highest levels of the force and they certainly didn't want to be unnecessarily implicated.

'Jesus and Esteban,' stated Ferran taking a more serious stance.

'I want you to know that anything you say to Jefe Perez Camps will not go any further without your knowledge and agreement. He is to be trusted. He is one of the best.' Jefe Perez Camps looked surprisingly bashful at this faint praise.

They both held their breath and then started to speak at the same time, nervously.

'Caballero and Sanchez,' they blurted out. Then laughed.

'You tell it Esteban,' instructed Jesus.

'Caballero and Sanchez are the two detectives implicated. We have statements from two dealers on tape.'

Jefe Perez Camps looked out of the window as he thought carefully about his words.

'It is disappointing. I had heard these names mentioned in connection with the lack of action on the Horta deaths. Tell me everything you have found out so far.'

Esteban and Jesus together went through the details of their findings. When they had finished they handed the Jefe a copy of the evidence tape.

'This is excellent work detectives. I will take this further and look into the level of corruption. This must be stamped out in the Mossos.' He got up to leave. As he said goodbye he paused momentarily and looked at Ferran.

'Ferran. I think you ought to know that Martes has been suspended. He was running a protection racket with a few major companies around the docks. He bit off more than he could chew.' Jefe Perez Camps winked at Ferran as he quietly relayed this information. Ferran smiled.

'I knew you would be pleased.' With that the Jefe strode purposefully off into Carrer Princesa.

Chapter 59

'Impressive man,' exhaled a relieved Jesus.

'Yeah. I'm exhausted from being on my best behaviour,' revealed Esteban. Ferran smiled, he understood their feelings, he had been there himself many years ago.

'You need not worry. He rates you both highly. Jefe Perez Camps is the best and most honest policeman you will ever meet. He will sort out the force.'

Ferran sipped his glass of wine, then drank some water.

'Now, I need your help. We need to move theses two cases on. They seem to have collided and I'm not totally sure we have got the right man. There are too many unanswered questions. As Conchita said, I really underestimated just how interesting and difficult the abduction case was going to be.'

'So, where do we start?' queried Jesus.

'Shall we note down everything we have so far,' suggested Esteban.

'Good idea, but I always prefer to talk things through. If we write it down then we have to read it again. Too much time is wasted writing rubbish,' Ferran pontificated.

Esteban understood and put away his ring bound note pad gingerly. He took the initiative in the conversation to regain some credibility in Ferran's eyes.

'What are the key points?' Esteban looked at the two detectives. They were lost in thought, so he continued lucidly.

'There were the four Horta murders.....three seem to have been committed by the husbands who then killed themselves, but the fourth remains unsolved.'

'But Jaume was involved in these wasn't he?' interjected Jesus, alert to the game they were now playing. This was enjoyable detective work.

'Yes, even though he was away at the time there is a possibility that he was involved. We have to consider this as his latest lover was also killed,' continued Esteban. Ferran was sitting back by now listening and thinking. He was impressed with his two young detectives.

'We need to re-open the Horta cases and look at them from scratch as we have found a link between all the women murdered and a therapeutic drugs group at the hospital, in which the Englishwoman, Sandie Shaw, who, of course, reported the abduction, was also involved,' added Jesus with some determination.

'Yes, don't forget that the drugs group was run by two people linked to drug dealers and implicating two corrupt detectives who have possibly covered up the outcome of the Horta killings,' continued Esteban. 'This may implicate the detectives, the drug dealers or the two hospital workers in the deaths of the women.' The two young detectives paused. They knew a fair amount about the Horta murders as they had been investigating. Ferran joined in.

'This is all very interesting. Remember, Jaume's first wife, the fourth Horta killing, was originally called Sandy Shaw, the same name as the woman Jaume met and who then claimed he had been abducted, Sandie Shaw.'

'This is really confusing,' confessed Esteban. 'Do you mind if I write some of it down?' He looked questioningly at Ferran. The Chief Detective smiled and nodded. Esteban pulled out his notepad and started jotting.

Ferran laid out more information they had gathered. 'Jaume claims that she is not Sandie Shaw but Lydia Bart. He apparently had an affair with her but has not seen for over six months.' Ferran leant forward on the table and rested his chin in his hands.

'So who is she? Lydia Bart, aka Sandie Shaw, who is she? There doesn't seem to have been an abduction of Jaume or a murder although forensics have found evidence of something going on at the Palau Sant Jordi.'

Jesus was thinking aloud, 'A body has turned up with Jaume's details on it, but it isn't Jaume. Why? Is it an insurance fraud?'

'It could be and who is the dead person? Was he murdered? Ferran asked.

'But what has the murder of Jaume's lover got to do with any of this?'

Esteban stopped writing as the three detectives fell silent. They were all thinking, trying to put these strands together. The wine bottle was empty.
'Do you two want a coffee? I need something to get my mind working,' muttered Ferran.
'Yes, please,' said Esteban.
'I'll get them,' Jesus said, as he called over the waitress.

Chapter 60

'So what have we got?' said Ferran out loud.
'What have we got to find out?'
They mused on the necessary courses of action.
'OK. This is what we need to do next,' instructed Ferran.
'One, investigate fully all four murder situations at Horta. Two, investigate any involvement of Jaume in the murder of his first wife or his lover. Three, further investigate the incidents at Palau Sant Jordi. Four, find out who Sandie Shaw/Lydia Bart is, her relationship with Jaume and why she claimed he was abducted. Five, investigate the murder of Jaume's lover. Less importantly, at this moment, six, find out how the old man carrying Jaume's papers died. And finally, investigate the drugs ring.' Ferran had raced through all that.
'Got all that down?' Ferran teased as Esteban continued to scribble.

Esteban looked up from his notepad, oblivious to the tease.
'Should we list the suspects? There is no doubt that all this is connected. Maybe if we fully investigate the suspects we will find our killer or killers.'
'I think you're right Esteban. Everything points to Jaume. It looks like he and the Englishwoman, Lydia or Sandie, whatever her name is, might be working together. Our first thoughts were that it

was an insurance scam. It still looks that way. Yet…..' He paused.

'Yet what?' asked Jesus.

'Did you really think that Jaume was a killer when you interviewed him earlier?' queried Ferran.

Jesus and Esteban both shook their heads.

'That's exactly how I feel. Instinct has a great deal to do with this job. You have to follow your instincts and my instinct says that Jaume isn't our man.' The coffee arrived and Ferran drank his cortado straight down and immediately ordered another.

'That's better.' He said as the caffeine took control of his nervous system.

'So who are our suspects? Get this down Esteban,' instructed Ferran.

Suspects:
- *Jaume – looks likely but instincts say not.*
- *Detectives Caballero and Sanchez – possible, but only if they have got too heavily involved in the drugs world.*
- *The two drug dealers – weak characters, but possible.*
- *The doctor and the male nurse from the hospital – possible but very unlikely, they were just out to make a little money and get free drugs.*
- *Someone we haven't yet thought of!*

Things were not getting any clearer. The restaurant was fairly empty now. It was mid-afternoon and a lot of people who had been in the restaurant had since returned to work.

'One person it could be...,' mused Ferran. 'Is the Englishwoman. It's very unlikely but we believe she is involved in this in some way, don't we?'

'We haven't met her,' said Jesus, speaking for Esteban and himself.

'What's she like? Could she kill?'

'I don't like her and I think she is completely mad, although it may all be an act. I can't make my mind up about her,' replied Ferran. He thought carefully about this for a second. Then he said. 'Add her to the list of suspects Esteban.'

They sat around silently for several more minutes. Then Ferran made a decision.

'I think you're right Esteban. Let's investigate the suspects. Jesus go back and dig up more on Jaume. I'll get Conchita to look into Lydia or Sandie, whatever her name is. I'll go and see how Maria is getting on with her, I'll find out if she has found anything out.' Ferran paused, then he looked at Esteban. 'Esteban. You look into the drug dealers and the two workers at the hospital. I'll also contact Jefe Perez to see what he's got on our two rogue detectives. OK?'

They nodded. Ferran got up, paid the bill and all three of them left the restaurant and headed off in different directions.

Chapter 61

It wasn't the best day to get through the city. Maria had thought it best to head up towards Gran Via as a quicker way to get to the seaside area of the city. It was an alternative to the busy port area at this time of year. She had badly misread the traffic though. Driving in Barcelona was, at best, tolerable, but the incessant traffic lights and grid after grid of tailbacks made even the most patient of drivers irate. She had taken the white, battered Seat up towards the Plaça de Catalunya and then headed off towards Carrer Trafalgar and on towards the Arc de Triomf. The traffic was crawling. Maria didn't like Ferran's Seat. She liked cars with air conditioning that worked and which gave a bit of pleasure when driven. She made a mental note to get him to upgrade when they were married. She didn't consider the car good enough or stylish enough for him anyhow. He would look much better in something like an Audi. She was hot and uncomfortable. Her passenger, who she had almost forgotten about, was sitting serenely, unphased by the traffic or the heat. The sun was blazing and Maria sweated, much to her annoyance, although Sandie Shaw sat motionless like an ice-maiden, immune to the heat.

The atmosphere in the car was reminiscent of a backstage situation before a Miss World competition. The two final contestants were incommunicado and the unspoken messages were unreapeatable. Maria tried to ignore the evil vibe that was starting to emanate from her passenger. She was trying to concentrate on the road and the traffic. Sandie Shaw was not looking at her driver, yet she was starting to focus all her negative energies towards her. Maria could feel it and she didn't like it. She didn't speak. She just wanted to get her back to her apartment and be rid of her.

She headed for the quiet road that skirted the bottom of the Ciuatadella Parc, hoping for less traffic. She was right. As she headed through the traffic lights onto the Passeig de Circumval Lacio there wasn't another car in sight. She planned to head up to the Olympic Village, turn right, head towards the seafront and down the Passeig Maritim into Barceloneta. She glanced across at her passenger. Nothing. No expression and no willingness to talk. She sensed her dislike, but she really didn't care. She focussed on the road and thought of the weekend ahead with her love, Ferran, planning their wedding. She smiled at the thought.

It happened so quickly. Sandie Shaw's right arm raced towards her head. Maria didn't see it coming. The palm of her hand connected with her brow and continued its momentum until it was halted by the glass of the drivers door. Her head smashed against the glass, instantly rendering her unconscious. The steering wheel looped around out of her hands. Her head lopped to the other side, falling on Sandie Shaw, who pushed it roughly out of the way. As she did so she slashed at her neck with the small kitchen knife in her left hand. It was an awkward position she was in and she didn't catch the detective as she had hoped. She saw the blood, though, as Maria's neck flopped towards the windscreen and rested on the steering wheel. The car had been in second gear and was not going particularly fast. Sandie Shaw clicked open the door and rolled out onto the road. She was a little bruised from the initial contact with the tarmac and her clothes were torn, but she stood on her feet and watched as the white Seat continued on its way. The car was veering across the road. There was nothing else around, but within seconds it had hit a wall and slammed to a halt. She saw Maria's body jackknife at impact. She turned and headed back towards the park. She felt nothing.

Chapter 62

Yellow lights hit her retinas. The lights hurt her eyes. She was sitting on the steps of the Estacio de França watching the traffic rush by. It was the ambulance lights that were making her wince and several of them flashed by. The station was quite quiet at this time of the day. Apart from her eyes she felt good. She was feeling invigorated. Life was good. She was looking forward to seeing Jaume again. She knew she wanted his children. They hadn't talked about it, although she was sure he would be keen. Spanish men love children. She felt sure he would like the idea. Where was he though?

She was feeling much brighter it was as if she was coming out of a mammoth hangover or migraine. Her eyes fixed on the Park Hotel. Just across from the station was this smart hotel where she and Jaume had spent their first few days in Barcelona together. The hotel was in the best possible location, not far from the sea and right in the middle of the tourist city. As she looked at the letters of the hotel's name that rose vertically above each other she visualised the comfortable room they had had that overlooked the station. Since then she had loved the Estacio de França. It was an art-deco feature to rank with the best. Well worth a visit in its own right. As she thought about it she was surprised there wasn't the usual camera crew filming a drama or documentary.

Her instincts were alert at last. She had been wondering where they had been over recent days. Her instincts told her not to go home. She could think of no reason why she shouldn't go home, but she just felt it would be wrong.
'Jaume won't be there,' she said out loud.
'After his abduction he won't want to go there. The memories will be bad. I can see that. He has my mobile number. He will contact me soon, then we can arrange to meet. It will be easier to get him home when we are together,' she thought. Logic convinced her not to go back to the apartment.

She stood up and crossed the wide road at the crossing. She passed the Park Hotel and settled down in an outside chair at one of the cafes that lined the Avinguda Marques de l'Argentera. Her stomach was empty and she needed refuelling. She ordered the 'ensalada del dia' and a beer. She was starving. As she waited for her meal to arrive she looked down at herself. She felt a little crumpled. Her dress she noticed was torn on the elbow and on her hip. This really perturbed her as she couldn't remember where this had happened. She tried hard but just couldn't find an explanation in her memory banks. She rode a bike regularly but she couldn't remember coming off it. That's what it looked like though. It looked as if she had had a fall and ripped her dress. There were sprinklings of blood on the front of her dress too. It looked like a spray of blood. Again, she had no memory. She decided to get herself sorted with a new set of clothes. She had fancied something expensive from Carhartt for sometime, and the shop was just around the corner. She decided to go just after her lunch.

Chapter 63

Two hours later she was dressed resplendent in brown. Brown long sleeved T-shirt, brown canvas pants, brown jacket and brown and cream converse sneakers. She felt good and expensive. The clothes were expensive. Her credit card was significantly damaged, but she felt good. She walked through Born. No, she paraded through Born, full of confidence and with an air of contentment. She felt good about herself. What man wouldn't want her? She could sense their eyes on her as she strolled past them. Even those with beautiful women on their arms gave her a second glance. This was how it was meant to be.

She strolled onto the Park Hotel. Room 21 was the one she wanted. It had been the room where she had spent several days with Jaume. It had been her first experience of Barcelona. What a time. What a city. They had stormed the place. La Paloma, Pla, Sagrada Familia, Barça F.C, Can Ramonet, and more. Best of all, they had had great, physical sex. Jaume was a great physical specimen. He was the fittest person she had ever had sex with. Her usual partners were often too drunk to perform perfectly, or was it her that was always too drunk? Jaume had a great body. He drank a little but he trained more. His muscles were well formed and his buttocks were tight. When he wore his toreador's jacket and hat she knew she was in for a treat. His penis was average size in her experience although when he dressed to his fetish he grew in stature. She loved it. She moaned as she remembered the impact on her body. She was surprised, as she had really pleasured herself with the thought of him. It felt almost as good as the real thing.

Room 21 was bare without a partner. She wandered around it, remembering. She needed sleep but she felt grubby. The shower was a pleasure she remembered, so she stripped off and enjoyed the experience again. Then she hit the bed and slept. As she dozed off she decided that this was the place for her until he returned. She didn't want to go home, not without Jaume. He would be back within a few days and then they would go home together.

Chapter 64

'I need to speak to you,' urged Conchita. He could tell from her voice that the issue was serious. Conchita didn't do serious well. She was full of life, of the living, full of fun.
'Why?' he asked, although he knew there would be a good reason, but that it would be a difficult question to answer.
'Ferran. I need to meet you quickly. Where are you?'
'I'm five minutes from you Conchita. Wait for me.'
He closed his Razr mobile and sped off towards the SIU office. What had happened? His mind worked incessantly delving through the possibilities. Was it to do with Maria? He hadn't spoken to her for a while, and these days she was the only thing that really mattered to him, she was his life. Conchita knew Ferran extremely well, so she would also know that any bad news about Maria would hit him hard. Deep down he knew her news was about his Maria. Conchita would want to be with him to give him some support.

His mind was flooded with grave images. It was like a cemetery after the plague. His face was ashen and he looked like he had aged ten years. He couldn't get the image of a dead Maria out of his head. Police work was dangerous and he knew she was always at risk, but she was smart, quick-witted and tough. He had never, in all their time together, worried about her in her work. She was the most careful police officer he had ever known. Her motto was to assess every risk before taking one and to always have an escape route. He felt like this when he had the news of his father's death. His father, a police officer, had been killed in a hostage situation at El Prat airport. Ferran had been very young but his stomach churned inside-out again as it does when you know you are never going to see a loved one again.

Nothing could happen to Maria. She was his life, his love, his soulmate. He had spent his whole life trying to find her and she was just beginning to give purpose to his life, at last, in his middle-age. What would he do without her? He stood still for a second. He had to compose himself. He told his mind to think positively. He didn't know what had happened to Maria. He didn't even know if the news Conchita had was about her. He started walking again and before too long he was at the SIU building. He raced up the stairs to the first floor office. He pushed his way heavily through the double doors. The crashed against the walls, the cushioning mechanism still hadn't been fixed. Ferran didn't care though. All he wanted was the news. His eyes searched out Conchita. She was sitting at her desk across the room. She wasn't smiling. She looked at him. He couldn't tell her mood, but she wasn't her usual self.

'It's Maria isn't it?' he asked. Conchita stood up and walked towards his stationary, rigid frame. He had never really noticed Conchita's body before as her vibrancy always directed you towards her personality. He couldn't help notice how commanding she looked. He felt very safe with this tall, slender, dark-skinned woman. She looked like one of the legendary 'Amazonians', tall, slim and strikingly attractive.
'Ferran. It is Maria, but she is going to be OK.'
'Going to be OK? What do you mean? Where is she? What has happened?' he spluttered. His agitation was clear.
'Calm down William.' She never called him William. No one ever called him William.
'She is going to be OK. She was attacked in her car and then it crashed into a wall. She's in the Hospital del Mar.'
'Attacked?'
'Cut with a knife. She has lost a lot of blood, according to her doctor, and she is unconscious but she is very lucky. The knife missed her artery. He says she will be OK with rest.'
Ferran stared at her. His face registered a little pleasure, as the news was not as bad as he had anticipated. He knew he had to be with her.
'Where's your car?'
'Outside.'
'Can I use it?' he told her.
'Yes, but I'm coming with you. I'll drive,' she retaliated.

Barcelona Betrayal

Conchita moved back towards her desk picked up her car keys from a jug on the top of her in-tray and rushed out of the doors with the detective.

Chapter 65

As they sat in the car, racing the short distance across the city to the hospital, Ferran frantically used his mobile trying to get through to the hospital to find out news. He was distraught. There was no one answering.
'Ferran. She will be all right. Just take it easy.' Conchita flashed him a worried look as she pushed the car to its legal limit along the broad city roads. Ferran wasn't listening. He was manic with worry.

As the car pulled up outside the hospital Ferran had the door open and was on the move before Conchita had even thought about putting on the hand-break. She placed her police-parking permit in the window and left it on the taxi rank right outside the main front entrance to the building. Conchita leapt out of the stationary vehicle and chased after Ferran. As she reached the centre of the main concourse in the hospital she caught sight of him at the hospital reception. He saw her and signalled with his right arm for her to follow. Conchita caught up with him and together they stepped into the elevator.

As they walked into the private ward Ferran tensed up. He didn't know what he was going to see. He couldn't imagine Maria in any state other than completely beautiful. He breathed in and paused at the door to the ward. Conchita was by his side. She squeezed his hand and then placed her hand on his back. She smiled at him as she pushed him forcibly into the room. She followed right behind him. Maria was lying motionless amongst the white sheets. She was unconscious but she still looked beautiful. Ferran stood just inside the door of the room. He was very tall, although at this moment he looked like a helpless little boy. He gasped gently. He looked at his future wife. She was gorgeous. Her face was bruised above her left eye, quite badly and her neck bore a twenty-centimetre scar. There were no stitches, just adhesive paper holding the skin together. She looked as if she was simply sleeping. Ferran moved forward and held her hand. At that moment the doctor on call waltzed, casually, into the room.

'Detective Ferran? This is your partner, yes?' He pointed towards Maria. Ferran nodded.

'You look worried. Don't be. I'll give you a 99% guarantee that she will be OK.'

'What?' queried Ferran. He looked confused.

'She had a lucky escape. No real problems. She is unconscious but our tests show that she will regain her senses within twenty four hours.'

'Will she be OK then?'

'No doubt. She just needs rest.' The doctor stood in his white overcoat with his hands in his pockets. Ferran walked over to Maria as the doctor and Conchita watched. He stood by the side of the bed and bent slowly over her. He kissed her gently on the forehead. She smelt like a hospital. He told himself to bring over her perfume. He stepped back slightly to look at her. To him she looked fine. He could feel her energy. He knew she would be OK. Conchita sensed his aura and knew what he had to do.

'Find out who did this. I will stay with her and let you know when she awakes.' Conchita was strong. He looked at her and then at Maria.

'Thank you, Conchita. You are a wonderful friend. Thank you. Let me know if anything at all happens here.'

'Don't worry Will, I will. I have your mobile number.' She held up her mobile in the palm of her right hand.

'And you can call me. I will be here.' She looked in control but relieved. Ferran sensed that she had been almost as worried as him, despite her reassurances. Seeing Maria in the flesh had relaxed then both. She was battered, bruised and unconscious, but she was going to be all right.

'Here, take my car.' She threw him the keys.

Chapter 66

'OK. So you have known Doctor Rafael Borrell Borras since you were at school. Is that right?' Jefe Perez Camps snorted as he paced around the interview room. The walls, floor and ceiling were white. There was only a table and two chairs in the room. A room that had seen many interviews and that could tell many stories. A tape recorder hummed on the white melanine table, picking up the words as they were thrown out by the three protagonists in the room. Sitting with his head sinking lower and lower between his legs was former detective Julio Caballero. 'Former' because he had been suspended and had pleaded guilty to the crime being investigated. There was no way back for him. He was co-operating to reduce his sentence. Walking around the room in a bigger circumference and anti-clockwise was the other investigative detective, Perez Camps's right hand man, the formidable Benvenuty. He had no first name, or at least no one knew it. Perhaps Perez Camps knew but he always referred to him as Benvenuty. He was medium build and medium height. Short, straight black hair, with not much receding despite his forty-plus years, and gelled down precisely. Like his boss, Perez Camps, he dressed impeccably. Today he wore a pink shirt, a red spotted tie and a plain black, spotless suit. His shoes gleamed. He didn't smile, ever. He said very little.

'Answer my question!' roared Perez Camps.
Caballero jumped slightly in response to the power of his voice. He sobbed.
'Yes. Yes. I have known him for twenty years or more.'
'Tell me, for the sake of the record, once again what your involvement was with the murdered women, Doctor Borrell Borras and his colleague David Garcia,' instructed Jefe Perez Camps as he strolled around the distraught former-detective in an ever-decreasing clockwise direction. His arms were behind his back and his hands clasped. He didn't look at Caballero or at Benvenuty, he just strolled on looking at the white floor.
'OK, OK. I really don't know Garcia well. We met him a few times, but he was really just moral support for Borrell Borras.'
'We?' said Perez Camps with a questioning emphasis.
'Yes. Sanchez and I did everything together.'
'So everything you are going to tell us now implicates you both. Yes?'
'Yes. We have been partners for ten years. I am married to his sister. We live in each other's pockets. He is like my brother.'
'Go on,' asserted Perez Camps.
'This all started about three years ago. We...Sanchez and me, were fed up with the treatment we were getting from the Mossos. We worked hard and got little back. We ran into Borrell Borras in a bar one night. He had a good

idea for making money. He ran rehabilitation clinics for drug abusers every night of the week. He had over forty patients. He knew that most of them had no intention of giving the things up but were really stressed-out in their day-to-day lives by having to raise the money to get the drugs and to then find reliable suppliers. He felt he could help them by providing safe, cheap drugs. He later got some of the women into prostitution to help them raise money.'

'Did you handle that?' interjected Perez Camps.

Caballero paused and thought. He was deciding which truth to tell.

'Yes. We managed the girls. Their customers were mainly from the Mossos.' Camps was repulsed by this thought. He stopped moving.

'Before we finish I want the name of every officer, who you are aware of, who took advantage of these women.' He was looking at Benvenuty and there was real steel in his voice. Caballero quivered with fear. He knew of the reputation of Benvenuty. Benvenuty said nothing but simply took a notebook out of his inside pocket and made a note of his task.

Chapter 67

'Continue,' snarled Perez Camps.
'We..we found a couple of reliable and safe dealers who would supply the drugs. They would meet the clients individually as they left the hospital. We would hang around and offer any protection. Not that much was needed. We took a share of the profits along with the doctor and his colleague.'
'So, how long did all this go on for?'
'Three years.'
'How much did you make?'
'With the prostitution as well, probably around €300-400 a week each.'
'Not a lot, but for about an hour's work a week, not bad. Did you have other similar scams?'
Caballero said nothing, but from his expression it was obvious he did.
'No worries. You can explain them all to Benvenuty later,' said Perez Camps with a smirk.
'Tell me about the Horta murders.'
'That wasn't us. Any of us,' Caballero said in a panic.
'You seem nervous. Why wasn't it any of you?'
'That is not our style. We didn't want to cut off the supply routes. With three of the couples, both the wives and their husbands had progressed onto heavier drugs, particularly acid. Their behaviour was changing because of their drug use. No one else was involved. Despite our involvement, our

investigations were very thorough and conclusive that no-one else was involved.'

'Are you sure? How do I know you are telling me the truth?'

'I know you. And I know…' Caballero glanced across at the other person in the room.

'I know Benvenuty.' He looked afraid. Perez Camps believed him, he looked terrified.

'So tell me about the Englishwoman. What did you find out about her death?' questioned Perez Camps.

'We obviously wanted to keep everything quiet and controlled so no one else would dig into all this and possibly find out about our involvement. The other deaths were not unexpected, they were all real addicts, almost degenerates. They weren't a surprise. The Englishwoman was different.'

'How?'

'She took drugs recreationally. She was at the clinic to try to stop taking them, but she wasn't really addicted. Her husband didn't touch them.'

'Was he involved in her death?'

'Absolutely not, he wasn't around much and at the time of her death he was in Madrid.'

'Yes, but could he have paid someone to kill her?'

'I don't think so. There was no reason. He had no insurance on her and he saw other women anyway. He was a real womaniser.'

'Jaume?'

'Yes. According to our investigations he slept with at least one different woman a week. He's a very attractive guy.'
'So who do you think killed her?'
'We really don't know. She slept around a lot too, especially when he was out of town. There were a lot of prints in their apartment. We checked a few of them out but there were no leads. The prints we found on the knife were very different.'
'What do you mean?' Perez Camps sat on the chair opposite the former detective. This was the first interesting thing he had said. Caballero paused. He was in full flow. He looked up at Perez Camps.
'We thought the prints we found on the knife belonged to a woman.'
Perez Camps looked at the floor. He stole a few minutes of silence.
'Why should I believe you? Where were you at the time of her death?'
'This is the absolute truth,' said Caballero as he looked the Jefe straight in the eyes.
'Sanchez and me were in Tarragona at the time of the murder.'
'Tarragona. Why?'
Caballero looked very sheepish.
'If I tell you will you keep your promise and be lenient with Sanchez and me?'
Jefe Perez Camps was not into deals.
'All I promised you was that you would not get hurt. I want you to get the justice you deserve. I hate crooked police. It is totally up to you what you

tell me. At this moment you are a murder suspect. Do you want to clear your name? Do you want me to leave the room and let my very good friend Benvenuty take over?'

Caballero was already pale faced but the thought of Benvenuty dealing with him flashed across his face. 'OK. We were in Tarragona buying a supply of impounded drugs from the Tarragona Mossos.'

Perez Camps face went crimson. He hated police corruption. He slammed his fists down on the table. The whole room shuddered. Caballero jumped, literally, several feet in the air. Benvenuty didn't flinch.

'I want the names of your contacts!'

Chapter 68

Bar Colombo on a late August midweek evening is a really mellow place to be. The temperature is fine and the clientele is mainly Spanish. A little too cool to sit outside but inside the bar it is quiet and hospitable. Tonight the dark haired, attractive, forty-something barmaid was in charge. Ferran didn't know her name but he liked her. She was strong-willed, looked after herself but looked like a lost soul. Ferran would have liked to have found out more about her in a previous life, but at this moment his mind was totally absorbed with his only love, Maria. He ordered a beer and sat at the bar. The waitress asked him if he was all right. He lied that he was. He needed to find out what had happened to Maria. He wanted to find her killer. First though, he needed a drink. He needed to think. Drink helped him think.

His last sight of Maria was at the morgue. She was with the very unpleasant Englishwoman, Sandie Shaw. She was about to take her home. He left her at about 10 a.m, surely she would have got rid of the Englishwoman well before the time the attack took place at about 1 p.m. He decided to phone Jefe Perez Camps. He would know what had happened. He dialled the number on his mobile with his thumb. His left hand held his second beer, his right hand his phone. The phone rang for a minute or so then clicked into the answer-phone. He tried the number again. After a few rings a big voice came on the end of the line.

'Hola, Perez Camps.'

Ferran was slightly surprised by the answer. He put his beer down and transferred the mobile into his right hand.

'Jefe. Ferran here.'

'Are you OK? How is Maria? I'm so sorry Ferran.'

Ferran had never heard his Chief so sympathetic. He knew the Chief liked him.

'She is going to be OK. She's unconscious but I've left Conchita with her. The doctor assures me that she will be fine.' He paused for breath.

'What I want, Jefe, is to find out what happened.'

'I have just come out of an interview room Ferran, so I don't know what has happened. Leave it with me for a few minutes and I will find out what knowledge we have. I'll phone you back.'

'Thank you Jefe.'

Chapter 69

Ferran placed both arms on the bar. His head hung low. He still looked very smart. His black velvet suit and white, open-necked shirt stood him apart from the other bar customers. He looked in crisis though. The bar was quiet and the barmaid obviously liked him. She looked concerned.
'Esta bien?'
He looked at her. He felt it ironic that someone so obviously confused about her own life would show concern for him. He liked her for it. She looked like she had plenty of issues of her own, yet she was concerned about his.
'Yes, but my partner is not so good..... I'm a little pre-occupied.'
'Vale. Can I help?'
'No, estoy bien.'
The waitress took the hint and retreated. Ferran's phone rang. He hauled it out of his pocket.
'Hola!'
'Ferran. Perez Camps here.'
'I have Detective Montserrat here, she was the officer who dealt with Maria's incident. Here she is.'
The phone rattled and Ferran waited patiently.
'Detective Ferran?'
'Si.'
'I was the first to arrive at the incident. Maria is now OK, yes?'
'Yes.'

Ferran couldn't imagine what Detective Montserrat looked like. Her voice was deep and shrill at the same time. Was she fat, tall, thin or young or old? He couldn't tell.

'She was alone when we found her. It was very quiet when the incident happened. There was no-one else in the car when we got there.'

'What about witnesses?' asked Ferran.

"No-one, except…,' she said.

'Except who?'

'Except a guy who said he thought he saw a woman walking away from the scene. He is not a good witness as he was at least 300 metres away from the incident.'

'What did he see?'

'He said he thought he saw a woman get out of the car whilst it was moving.'

'Is that it?' queried Ferran.

'Si, Detective Ferran.'

'Thank you,' replied Ferran.

He had an instinctive feeling for what had happened. He ordered another drink and thought carefully about his next move.

Chapter 70

The ceiling moved. Yes, it was definitely moving, she was very sure. The ceiling was rotating. What was going on in her head? She needed something to settle her mind. She managed to roll over slightly on the bed and fumbled for her purse. Her right hand knocked a glass of water off the bedside cabinet. There was little left in the glass. It fell limply on to the rug that covered most of the marbled floor. Her hand pursued the errant purse. Moments later she trapped it, rolled onto her back and held the purse steady above her head. She was trying to focus on its contents. Two coins hit her on the forehead as she fumbled inside the now opened purse. She found what she was looking for and casually discarded the purse. The tab in her hand slipped easily under her tongue. Just the process of putting it in her mouth made her feel better. Within a few minutes she felt in control. Her mind was expanding. She reminded herself that Jaume was coming to see her at the hotel. It was time to make herself look and feel good. She gradually stripped off her clothes. Slowly. Carefully exploring each item of clothing with her eyes and her fingers as she removed them. She was fascinated by the texture and the look of them. As each item was taken off she laid the clothes on the side of her bed. Within several minutes she was naked. Her hands slowly roamed her body. She felt good about herself. Her image in the mirror on the wall was pleasing to her. Her weight was too heavy, but only slightly.

The shower refreshed her. The water powered onto her head, spraying off it onto the rest of her body. It was warm and cleansing. Her mind alternated between total clarity of how life would soon be between Jaume and herself and total confusion. Confusion was gradually settling in. She shook her head. Clarity returned. Jaume would be here within thirty minutes. What should she wear? It was important to impress. She didn't have much with her. Her new clothes would have to do. The shower was now irrelevant. What was important was the look. She wanted a look to recapture her lover, her lover, Jaume. He was coming home. She couldn't wait.

She was dressed and ready. The bed held her up. Her body was prone and relaxed. Had he said he would meet her at the hotel, or where? She couldn't remember. As she lay on the bed she played through the possible scenarios for their long-awaited reunion. The confusion in her mind was less, she felt relaxed. Tiredness filled her limbs. The energy was draining away from her. The initial rush from the tab had ebbed away. She closed her eyes.

Chapter 71

It was dark when she opened her eyes. For a moment there was panic in them. Where was she? Her body was tense and defensive. The realisation of where she was hit her as suddenly as the flow of calmness that rippled through her senses. She felt rested and her mind was lucid. The table lamp to the left of the bed was just visible. It clicked on easily. As she lay back on the bed it wasn't long before she noticed her clothes. She was fully dressed. Her sleep hadn't disturbed the neatness of what she was wearing. She still looked good. Her mouth felt dry and in need of something fresh. The roll off the bed was accomplished with ease and her limbs felt relaxed and rested. The light brown bedspread matched the cool creams and browns of the room. Her bare feet scuttled across the reed woven rug onto the cool, marble floor of the bathroom. It was startlingly white. Everything shone with white freshness in the brightness of the bathroom. The toothpaste brought instant relief to the crust of staleness in her mouth. As she brushed her teeth she surveyed her general appearance in the mirror on the wall.

'Not bad for an old bird,' she laughed to herself. Her hands carefully adjusted her hair and straightened her clothes.

'Where is he?' Her voice was disappointed.

'Anyone would think that he was trying to avoid me.' She stood staring at herself in the mirror. Her brain was ticking over. Considering her options. What should she do next? It wasn't long before her thought mechanisms had come up with an outcome.

'I need to see you Jaume. I can't think why you haven't turned up.' She was getting agitated. Then a thought occurred to her.

'Maybe something has happened to him?'

Her phone buzzed. She jumped. The phone was in her pocket. There was a message. She flipped open the cover and read it.

'I need to talk 2 u. Jaume. Meet at Café Born asap.'
Without a moment's hesitation she raced out of the bathroom, hurriedly put on her shoes and left the hotel room. Within minutes she was marching along Avinguda Marques de l'Argentera under the light of the moon and assorted streetlights.

Chapter 72

The early evening darkness had emptied the bar. Ferran sat on his stool drinking his third beer and thinking.
'Ferran? Jesus here.'
'Si, Ferran.'
'Is Maria OK? I've just heard the news. Is she alright?' Jesus was perturbed and insistent.
'Yes, yes, Jesus. Don't worry. I have seen her and Conchita is with her. She is fine. Conchita phoned me a few minutes ago. She is stirring a little. I'm sure she will soon be awake and ordering us all around,' he joked bravely.
'That is good Detective Ferran, very good news indeed.'
'What news do you have Jesus? Have you found out any more about Jaume?'
Jesus hesitated on the phone.
'I'm not sure if it is good or bad news Detective Ferran. I think it makes things less clear.'
'What have you found out?' insisted Ferran.
'I haven't found anything out, but the news is that Jaume is about to be released from Gran Via.'
'Why?' Ferran was shocked.
'The pathologists initial report states that Christina Reia La Portes was killed at around midday. Jaume has claimed his innocence throughout, and the CCTV cameras at the hospital confirm that he was in the hospital all day, from about 8 a.m through to late afternoon. He couldn't have killed her. He may

have paid someone to do it but we have no evidence.'

'But that is two of his women that have been killed in this way. He must surely be involved,' snapped Ferran.

'It looks that way, but there is no evidence. Like you, I don't believe Jaume killed either woman. I think he loved them both,' replied Jesus.

'I think you are right Jesus. I really don't think it is Jaume, he did really love Christina, I am sure, and probably his wife.'

'What about the detectives and the drug pushers? Could it be them?' enquired Jesus hopefully, looking for an alternative suspect.

'I really don't think so. Perez Camps is working on Caballero and he has Detective Benvenuty with him.' He paused for Jesus to understand his implication. Jesus sighed. He had already heard of the reputation of Benvenuty.

'So you see, Caballero will tell the truth and it seems that they were not involved in murder,' continued Ferran.

'Who does that leave?' queried Jesus.

'Well I have a feeling. I don't want to say more just yet. But, maybe this is all just beginning to make sense. Jesus, I need you to follow Jaume when he is released. Get Esteban to help you. This is very important. I think he may be in danger. He must be watched around the clock. Work it out with your colleague, but don't let Jaume know you are there. Understand?'

'Yes, but...,' stuttered a confused Jesus.
'Just do it Jesus, I will explain my thinking later. Adios.' Ferran closed his Razr phone, paid the bar bill and left Bar Colombo. He hit the Passeig de Maritim and joined the holidaymakers, beach creatures and restaurantgoers along the seafront as he headed back towards the Hospital del Mar.

Chapter 73

The seafront was busy with people as Ferran hurried along walking as fast as he could. He loved this part of the city. He just couldn't believe how it had changed during his lifetime. When he was younger, before the Olympic redevelopment of the city, Barceloneta and the seafront was generally a no-go area for the likes of middle class families, such as his. The old seafront chiringuito restaurants were popular but not for the respectable middle classes. Further down the coast towards the Forum area, near Besos, he remembered the smells associated with what could only be described as a shanty town. Many of the immigrants who had arrived in the sixties and seventies from the south lived in home-made shacks. His father had taken him to the area once when he was very young. He had never found out why. They had just driven slowly around the area. At the time Ferran was going through a difficult and lazy time in his early teenage years and he felt his father was trying to show him what would happen to his life if he didn't work. As he was remembering this he suddenly, for the first time, realised what his father was doing through that visit. He saw it like a vision, as if his father was now, after all these years, explaining it to him. He had wanted Ferran to see the suffering of humanity, he had wanted the young boy to feel emotion for the less privileged people in the world, he had wanted Ferran to spend his life trying to make a difference. He realised suddenly that that visit his father had taken him on to the Besos shanty town, had formed the subsequent basis of his life. He had always wanted to make a difference. He abhorred corruption and privilege. He felt humbled by the memory as he walked along. The seafront at night made him think of all these things. The smells, atmosphere and lighting acted like a time-bank and stirred up lost memories. He hurried on his way.

A strong wind was building off the sea as he reached the hospital. The air had turned chilly and he was pleased to get inside the entrance to the hospital building. It wasn't long before he reached Maria's private room. He gently opened the door. Conchita was sprawled out on the floor on top of several towels to give some comfort. She was fast asleep. He looked at Maria. The tubes and drips cluttered his view but he quickly focussed on her face. Her colour had returned. He stepped over to her and kissed her gently on the lips. She stirred. He stepped back watching her murmurings. She fidgeted and pulled a contorted face at him. Slowly her eyes opened. She focussed on him.
'Will. Will. Oh, Will.' She limply held out her arms. He gently embraced her and their lips met. It was probably the most wonderful and most meaningful kiss either of them had ever had. It was an electric moment. Emotions whizzed between them. At that

moment they both knew they would never be parted. Eventually they broke free of each other. Ferran stood back and looked at his love.

'Wow!' Which was probably his favourite word, was all he could say. Maria smiled and reached out for his hand. Ferran held it and sat on the chair next to the bed. They just stared at each other mistily for several moments.

'Maria! Oh, thank goodness,' Conchita cried out as she appeared from on the floor. She was delighted to see her friend and colleague awake. The next few minutes were spent in frenzied and tiring conversation between the three of them. It was as if Maria had been away for six months.

When all the emotional feelings had subsided Maria was obviously exhausted and ready for more sleep. Ferran had business on his mind.

'Maria, before you rest some more. Tell me. Was it Sandie Shaw, the Englishwoman who did this to you?' He looked at her enquiringly. Maria looked at him and smiled.

'You are so good Ferran, how did you know?'

'Later Maria, I will tell you later. I must go now.' He kissed her on the forehead, waved to Conchita and hurried out of the room. He had to act quickly.

Chapter 74

'Jesus,' Ferran snapped as the mobile was answered.
'Where are you?'
'I am with Esteban. We are sitting in the Café del Born keeping an eye on Jaume.'
'What is he doing?'
'Sitting at the bar drinking. He looks like he is trying to forget his life!' replied the young detective.
'Tell me if you move off. I will try to join you as soon as I can.' With that Ferran rang off.

The Café del Born was a cool hangout. Esteban and Jesus really liked it. Whenever they were in this part of the city they would meet friends here. It was a meeting place for young, culturally aware Catalonians. Tonight the place was buzzing. There were twenty or so people chatting and drinking in the tall, narrow room. The place was hard to describe as it wasn't old and wasn't new. It was sparse and comfortable. The floor-to-ceiling red wooden shutters at the front of the building gave it a distinct feel. Apart from the shutters the place was indistinct, yet it had character. The two detectives couldn't understand why Jaume had ended up at the cafe, as it just didn't seem to be his kind of place at all. Yet it had been obvious from his actions that he had intended to go there. It wasn't an accident.

The two young detectives had had a very long day. They looked dishevelled and tired. They sensed though that this case was heading towards a climax. Something was going to happen and they both wanted to be there when it did. Sleep could wait. They sipped their beers and chatted. Jesus was occupying the time by relaying to Esteban his view on the qualities of the younger females in the café. He was confident and successful with women. Esteban was shy with them. Jesus had a mission to find Esteban a mate.

They kept a watching eye on Jaume. He sat at the tall wooden bar and drank. His nose was in his glass as he hunched over his beer. He wasn't drinking quickly but he was on his third beer. He didn't seem to be waiting for anyone. He was just looking into his glass and, every now and then, drinking from it. He seemed oblivious to anyone. He certainly hadn't noticed the two detectives. They had positioned themselves at the rear of the café, almost hidden from his view by several tables of people.

Chapter 75

Jesus was busy making eye contact with a brunette with a figure he wanted to explore. Her stomach was exposed, revealing an interesting tattoo. He was fascinated and wanted to find out more. She noticed his interest and whenever her boyfriend was distracted made it obvious with her eyes that she was interested. He scribbled his mobile number on a piece of newspaper and was about to surreptitiously hand it to her when he noticed Ferran creep into the bar. Ferran saw Jaume sitting at the bar and kept his eyes on him, prepared to take evasive action if seen, as he sought out the two young detectives.

Ferran pulled up a chair and sat with Esteban and Jesus.
'Maria is OK? Yes?' queried Esteban immediately.
'Yes. She is awake now. She will be fine in a few days time.'
'Who attacked her?' asked Jesus. 'Did she say?'
Ferran was about to reveal his thinking to them with his mouth open poised to speak when he noticed the woman walk into the café.
'Look.' He pointed to the door. At the same time trying not to be seen.
'It's her. Sandie Shaw!' The three detectives stared in amazement. Jaume and Sandie Shaw together. Ferran's thinking changed again. Maybe they were in all this together after all? Perhaps she was

actually telling the truth? Why on earth would they be together? He had said he hadn't seen her for months.

Her eyes had settled on Jaume sitting at the bar immediately. She saw no one else. Her manner was exuberant. She looked good and she was smiling and full of life. As she walked up behind Jaume he hadn't noticed her entrance. She kissed him on the back of the head. His right hand instinctively shot up as a form of defence as he swung around to face her. His expression belied his feelings. He wasn't pleased to see her. She wore disappointment across her face. The reaction of her lover Jaume was not what she had expected. Where was the kiss? The long awaited embrace and the sparkling smile? Instead all she got was a frown and a mumbled invitation to sit down. What she didn't read from his expression was his intense dislike of her. He hated her. He could hardly bear to speak to her. Without looking at her he ordered her a beer. His gaze was towards the back of the bar. She sat perched on her stool facing him, confused but just pleased to be with him.

'Why did you do it?' he said towards the array of spirit bottles that formed a glass wall at the rear of the bar.
'Sorry?' She hadn't heard his mumble.
'Why did you do it?' he repeated with venom.
'Why did I do what?'

'Kill them.' She was shocked. Her body language changed to the defensive. The three watching detectives were fascinated, their eyes hardly daring to blink as they soaked up every instant of the action.

'Kill who?' she questioned.

'My women, why did you kill my women? I must know.' He turned and looked at her. His eyes were obsessed with pure, undiluted hatred. They bore into her. She reeled back slightly.

'Jaume. I love you. I only want you and I to be together. We are so good together. You must forget about your other women. This is our city, this is our love, this is our life. Come with me. Let's continue where we left off. I have been waiting for you to come home.' It was as if she had rehearsed these words many times. She smiled a sickeningly sweet smile as she finished speaking. Jaume just stared at her in disbelief. In the end he looked away. Then he spoke quietly to her.

'I have never loved you. I will never love you. I will never forgive you for what you have done.'

'Jaume. I don't understand why you are being like this.' She reached out to put her hand on his knee. He repelled the advance by pushing her hand away.

'I asked you here because I needed to get some understanding on what has happened to my life,' he gasped in an exhausted voice. It was clear that she was not registering any empathy with his thought waves. It was as if he was speaking another language backwards.

'Our apartment is close. Let's go back there together. Come on Jaume.'

His look said it all. The mere thought of being naked next to her totally repulsed him.

'Who are you?' he rasped.

'I thought you might be humane enough to give me some answers, but I can see you are a totally self-obsessed, selfish and completely mad woman. I never ever want to see you again. Get away from me now before I am forced to do something I will regret.' His voice and manner made it clear that he meant what he said. She reflected for a moment. She didn't like the way he was speaking but she took it. The three watching detectives observed an instant character transformation in the woman as they watched. They saw the sickeningly sweet, doe eyed love object turn into a hard-edged, emotionless being. She stared menacingly back at Jaume. He looked up at her. He flinched as he caught her stare.

'If you don't want me Jaume I will not let you have anyone else. I will expect you back at the apartment tonight. If you don't come, I will assume that you are prepared to suffer the outcome of your misguided and rash decision.' As she laid down this ultimatum she got off the stool and headed out of the bar. Jaume was stunned and just a little unnerved.

'Wait....' Too late, she was gone.

Ferran looked at Esteban and Jesus. What a show. They had heard or lip-read every word. Ferran sparked into action.
'Follow him. Don't let him out of your sight. Keep me informed by phone. I'm after her.' With those words he dashed across the room, skirting the loose chairs and tables, before he disappeared out of the bar into the evening darkness.

Chapter 76

The tourist traffic was heavy that night in that particular part of Born. It was as if several coach loads of experienced tourists, devoid of spatial awareness and with a tendency to all move in different directions, had been unloaded on the Carrer de Comerç at the same instant. Ferran ran straight into them. The scrum of elderly tourists resisted his movement for a few minutes before he ploughed through them. He had seen her move off towards the Estacio de França as she had left the Café del Born. Where was she now? He escaped the melée of tourists and stood exhausted. His eyes were searching every street and every doorway. Where was she? He couldn't see her anywhere. He ran off towards the most obvious direction he felt she would have taken. She had appeared deranged and wouldn't necessarily do the expected, although it was worth a try. He reached the Avinguda Marques de l'Argentera and stood facing the Estacio de França. He searched the whole of the wide, tree-lined street. She wasn't there. He rested for a moment with his hands on his hips. He reached up and loosened his shirt. The top button was already open. He opened two more buttons to let the air into his hot body.

She saw him race by her. The tourists had been a welcome diversion. She had seen Ferran in the bar. She had recognised the man she had hated most in this world, the man who had given her such a torrid time in the police interview room. She knew what she would like to do to him, but not now, later. Her mind clicked forward. There was now a man she hated even more than Detective Ferran. This man had spurned her. He was a man who had turned to other women ahead of her. A man she wanted to punish. Jaume. Her body stood rigid in the shadows. She loved her ability to act coolly in difficult situations. She wasn't phased by anything. As she had come out of the bar she had kept close to the buildings, avoiding the tourists and found an unused, dark doorway. It was unlit and anonymous.

Ferran was frustrated. He went back towards the Café del Born looking for a possible lead on the direction she took. He stood right in front of a dark doorway, looking out across Carrer de la Ribera. She stood stark still in her darkness behind him. She didn't breathe. He didn't know his prey was standing a few metres away from him. She felt like punishing him. After all he was within reach of her and he wouldn't stand a chance. He didn't know she was there. She was tempted. She reached inside her jacket. Her right hand felt the handle of the blade. It would be easy. As she wound her hand and fingers around the handle and waited for the right moment he dashed off in the direction of the café. The adrenalin that was building in her body was released. She stood still and relaxed. Now, all she had to do was wait.

Chapter 77

Was he still there? Ferran wasn't sure if Jaume would still be in the bar. He carefully approached the Café del Born and peered around the edge of the red shutters. He was still at the bar. His head was still resting just above his beer, supported on his arms, with his elbows on the bar. Esteban and Jesus were still watching his every move. Ferran manoeuvred his way to the back of the room to join them.

'Where is she?' asked Jesus.

'I never found her. She just disappeared,' replied Ferran.

'Tell us what you think is going on,' suggested Esteban. Ferran looked very dishevelled. His usual cool was elsewhere. He was frustrated at losing her and he wasn't sure what was going to happen next. All he knew was that he had to find her.

'Esteban. I will tell you, but first could you go outside and phone through a message to the Mossos to pick up Sandie Shaw, aka Lydia Bart, give them a description. Tell them it is high priority.' Ferran sat back in the chair and finished his beer. He was exhausted. It crossed his mind that he wasn't quite as young as he thought he was.

'I've done that Detective Ferran. The Mossos and the Guardia are looking out for her,' reported Esteban as he rejoined them.

'Now tell us what is going on,' repeated Esteban.

Ferran looked at Jaume to check he was still there. Then he told the two young detectives what he thought.

'Sandie Shaw or Lydia Bart is the killer of Jaume's wife, Sandy Shaw, and his lover, Christina Reia La Portes.'

'Why?' queried Jesus in amazement.

'I'm not totally sure yet, although I am sure that her relationship with Jaume, apart from an initial few months together, is totally imaginary.'

'What? Even the abduction and supposed murder at Palau Sant Jordi?' commented an amazed Jesus. Esteban was too surprised to speak.

'Yes. She may even have gone back to make it look like it had happened, although I'm not too sure about that part of my theory.' He paused. He looked at the eager eyes of the two young detectives. If he hadn't been so concerned about the location of the missing woman he would really be enjoying this, he loved telling a story. 'It's a type of schizophrenia,' he continued. 'Many years ago I came across a similar case in Girona. The man in that case believed that he was living a very different life for most of his time. Sandie Shaw is Sandy Shaw, Jaume's lover, for half of her time. For the rest of her living space she is Lydia Bart. She doesn't remember the second life when she is the other person. Understand?' The two young detectives were very tired but they were also extremely interested in what was happening.

'Yes, it all makes sense. But what made you think it was her?' questioned Esteban.
'We don't know for definite that it is yet. But when we couldn't imagine Jaume killing, and with the other obvious suspects also discounted, I was left with her as the only possibility. Then I remembered the previous case and I started to imagine how she was feeling. My view was confirmed when Maria said she was attacked by Sandie Shaw.'
Esteban and Jesus were shocked. They hadn't been aware of that.
'She is very dangerous. We must find her.'
The three of them slumped back in their wooden chairs. It was quite late and they were all exhausted. No one spoke. They all just looked up at Jaume through the now packed bar. At that moment he paid and moved off.

The surprise movement held them back momentarily. Esteban hung around to pay for their drinks whilst Ferran and Jesus followed Jaume out of the bar.

Chapter 78

His direction was the Estacio de França. Jesus crossed the Caller de Comerç and Ferran hugged the buildings on this side. They were careful not to be seen. Jaume was stumbling along slowly. Ferran glanced back towards the Café del Born and saw Esteban racing to join them.

She saw Jaume from close quarters. He walked straight past her. He was inches away. She knew he wasn't going back to their apartment. She sensed it. That was it then. She had to act. There was no alternative. He deserved nothing better. She started to move out of the shadows when she saw Esteban catching up with Ferran.
'Bugger,' she said to herself quietly. 'There are three of them.' She hadn't realised. She had only observed Ferran talking to another person earlier. She checked herself and was very careful before she moved off out of the shadows in pursuit of Jaume.

As he approached the station its edifice rose up above him. It was a supremely grand station. The façade was pure art deco and resplendent 1930's. Night blanketed the city and the streets were busy. The road teemed with taxis and cars. The pavements heaved with people seeking out food and entertainment. Jaume waited patiently at the crossing in front of the station. The green man took an age to arrive. His pursuers held their pace, and from a cautioned distance, waited too. Eventually the lights changed. Jaume crossed and pounded up the few steps into the station. The detectives were held up as the lights changed to red. They didn't notice that, 50 metres along the avenue, a woman swept across the road skirting around the oncoming traffic. She disappeared into the station shortly after Jaume, but unnoticed through another entrance.

The station concourse was like no other. The huge, grand hallway was decked in marble stone and was a truly resplendent sight Ferran paused, he had always been taken a little aback by the sight of this wonderful station. He quickly corrected himself and went in pursuit of Jaume. Esteban and Jesus were first into the main area of the station where there were trains. Only two platforms had trains waiting to leave. They hurriedly looked up at the computer screens that showed departures. One train was heading for Valencia and one for Girona. The three detectives stood together beneath the screen just inside the platform area of the station. They searched with their eyes for a glimpse of Jaume.

Chapter 79

It was late. This was the last train to Girona. He had a friend, Simon, in the city. He was determined to start afresh. Girona was Catalonia, he loved Catalonia, but it was far enough away from Barcelona for him to forget. The carriage was empty. He had chosen an empty carriage. He really didn't want to talk to anyone. He had had plenty of choice. Most of the carriages were empty.

He paced up and down a short section of the passageway between the seats in the carriage. He was very agitated. The meeting with her had not gone as planned. He wanted to know if she had been responsible. He hadn't been at all sure. He was now. That was what bothered him. Was he safe? He thought about that for a moment. He didn't really care. He had loved his wife Sandy Shaw but they had been going through a rocky patch when she was killed. They had both wanted other people and had both slept with other people. Their relationship was at an end. He had loved her, but he hadn't missed her. Christina was very different. He had loved her with all of his soul. She was a beautiful person and had a wonderful personality. He had wanted to spend his life with her, every waking moment of it. Her death was a savage blow to him. What was the point in carrying on? He had wanted revenge but then thought about the point of that. His thought processes had led him to simply want to understand. At this moment in time he really didn't understand why someone had taken her away from him. How could someone kill another person? He felt as if life was cheap and worthless. He paced around the carriage.

On his release from the Mossos he had wanted to get revenge, that at least was his first thought. He had spent hours thinking of the likely suspects. Every time he came back to Lydia Bart. He had no enemies, he was a nice guy. Few, if any, people disliked him. She was his big mistake. He could understand why she would do it. He didn't think it would be her though. She would get someone to do her dirty work. His mind had been racing. If he met her and she had admitted it he was going to kill her. That was clear in his mind. His thinking had been lucid enough for him to pop into his friend Lucio's apartment on Carrer de Trafalgar on his way along from Gran Via. Lucio was paranoid about robbers and kept a small revolver in his apartment. He had bragged to Jaume about it many times. He knew where it was and he knew where Lucio kept a spare key. He had quickly picked up the gun on the way to his meeting with her at the Café del Born. During their short time together they had regularly sat there over a beer. He knew she would come.

In the end she didn't admit to the murders although he sensed she was responsible. He didn't have the nerve to take her out. His idea was fine in principle, but in reality he wasn't up to it. Instead he would run away and make a new life for himself. He paced along the carriage. His hands were dug deep into his jacket pockets, his eyes piercing into the metal floor. All of a sudden he knew he wasn't alone. He sensed another presence in the carriage. Someone was behind him. He turned around and looked up. There she was.

'Jaume. Where are you going? You were meant to be joining me in our apartment. Weren't you?' Her words were like rigid steel rods. They hit him like iron darts. He felt winded. She walked towards him. He was terrified. She didn't seem human. There was nothing but pure evil in her eyes. Something glistened in her hand. It was something small. He stared and stared. It was a knife. The knife was no more than a small kitchen blade but it was held with intent. It was jutting upwards at a forty-five degree angle from her right hand. The blade glistened in the carriage lights, as if it was sending out a warning message in morse code. As she slowly continued towards him she spoke again.

'Jaume, speak to me. You are a bad man and you need to be punished. Your life is with me and with me only. You have no other option.' She increased her pace and was within centimetres of him when she raised her hand. The knife flashed towards his neck.

The expected pain didn't hit him. Instead he felt a shudder and a loud explosion emanating from his waist. Her neck exploded. Blood splattered the carriage and she reeled helplessly backwards before her legs crumpled beneath her. Jaume was horrified. He looked on as the blood flooded out of her harmless body, as it lay motionless on the carriage floor.

Chapter 80

Ferran, Esteban and Jesus stopped moving as they heard the shot. Their ears told them where it had come from. They raced towards platform two, unbuttoning their guns from their shoulder holsters as they went. The noise had come from the fourth carriage along.

Jaume leaned back against a seat. What had happened? He looked down at his jacket. A black smouldering hole had replaced the pocket. His hand came out of the pocket remotely. He had lost control over his actions. In his hand was Lucio's gun. He looked down at Lydia. The blood had stopped pumping out of the neck wound. The life had left her body. He felt strange. He saw nothing. The lifeless hulk looked just like a lifeless hulk. He registered no emotion, nothing. He wasn't pleased and he wasn't sad. He looked at the gun. Without thinking he held it to his head and he started to pull the trigger for a second time.

Ferran was outside the carriage on the platform. He saw what was about to happen. He banged on the window and shouted, 'Noooo!' At the same time Esteban entered the carriage at the far end. He shouted to Jaume to put the gun down. Jaume didn't hear him. He pulled the trigger.

The three detectives quickly leapt inside the carriage and were racing towards Jaume. Too late! They flinched as they heard the click of the gun. The explosion never came. Jaume looked at the gun. Why hadn't it fired? As he looked at it again Esteban tackled him and knocked him to the ground, making sure the gun was released out of his grasp.

Jesus pounced on Jaume and quickly searched him as he lay hurting on the carriage floor. When he was sure he was unarmed he pulled him up and sat him on a double seat, at all times holding his gun over him. He had no trouble. Jaume looked empty. He stared into space. He looked as if he didn't know where he was, he certainly didn't care. Esteban got to his feet and picked up Jaume's gun from under a seat. He handed it to Ferran. The Chief Detective looked at it and then opened up the barrel. Inside it was empty. There had only been one bullet in the gun.

Chapter 81

The piece of meat on the plate carried by the waiter was enormous. There was little space left on the ceramic for accompaniments. The juices were flowing out of the seared meat. It looked delicious.
'That can't be mine,' howled Maria in feigned horror.
'Si, esta para tu, Señorita,' returned the waiter. He placed the huge sirlon steak down in front of her. Her mouth watered just at the sight of it.
'Your doctor told me you needed a week of raw meat in order to get your red blood cells back to normal,' smiled Ferran.
'What better pace than El Paraguyo? If you want meat, this is the place.' As he spoke his own huge T-bone steak was placed, steaming, in front of him.
Maria smiled at her lover, her man, her hero and her husband-to-be. Ferran loved her. His love was enhanced following her near death experience. He had known he had loved her but the fear of losing her had made his love a certainty. He looked at her. She was pale but she looked great. Her face had healed and there was no sign of the scar on her neck beneath the make-up Maria had expertly applied.

El Paraguyo was busy. If you came in late you had to have booked a table. Ferran had thought ahead. Not far from Las Ramblas and the main Passeig De Colom on Carrer Parc, this small wood panelled restaurant was a jewel. The food was threatening to vegetarians but it was good. Ferran reached across the small table and took hold of Maria's delicate but strong hand.

'So, Maria, you gave me a real scare. We need to get married before you do it again. Then at least I can brag to people about having been married to the wonderful and beautiful Maria Fernandez Tupelo.' He smiled at her.

'That's very morbid Will. Anyway I will be Maria Fernandez Ferran I think.' She caught his eyes with that wicked but insistent look he so loved.

'Let's talk marriage later. You are not going anywhere Will Ferran. Consider yourself well and truly snared.' They both laughed the kind of laugh only associated with two people madly in love with other.

'Tell me about the investigation. What was the outcome?' Ferran was surprised.

'Are you sure you want to talk in that order? Not marriage first?' he joked.

'Get on with it, tell me.' They both settled down to attack their slabs of meat.

'Jaume was guilty of nothing other than killing Lydia Bart. That was in fact her real name.'

'What will happen to him do you think?'

'A prison sentence, but not that long. He may even get away with a suspended one. He is harmless, he shouldn't have had the gun but he shot her in self-defence and he had undergone an intense mental breakdown having lost both his loves. His psychiatrist is very good. She will do her best for him in court. I doubt that he will ever again be the man he was.'

'It is very sad. How a life can be so changed by a chance meeting. What did you find out about Lydia Bart?'

'Yes, her meeting with Jaume was by chance. It was through the dating small ads in a London paper. Jaume was looking for sex and she was looking for love. Conchita has been in touch with the Metropolitan police and they were very helpful. Lydia Bart had no criminal record, other than for being drunk and disorderly when she was younger, but she did have psychiatric records.'

'Really? What kind of things?' asked Maria with her mouth full of steak. Ferran considered the paradoxical picture of beautiful Maria with a piece of steak hanging out of her mouth as she spoke. Then he refocused on the question.

'She had suffered severe mental stress. The notes relate to problems with her parents and in developing meaningful, loving relationships. She just wanted to be loved but, by the look of things, she had never received any. Her father killed himself when she was in her teens, so there was a history of mental illness in the family. Also....'

'Go on,' urged Maria. 'This is really interesting.'

'From her late teens she was a regular user of 'entertainment' drugs.'

'What? Such as ecstasy?'

'Yes, and more prevalently, LSD.'

'I'm not surprised she was living in fantasyland then,' commented Maria.

'It appears that Jaume couldn't get rid of her in London and so he finished his course early in London and came back to his wife in Barcelona. He was weak and, rather than finish with Lydia in London, he thought that she would just forget about him.'

'I suppose with her mental state he may have been a little worried about what she might do to herself.'

'It appears that way. I think he was also worried about what she might do to him. There is a police record about an incident, an argument where they were called to their flat in London where she had attacked him with a kitchen knife. It wasn't major but it shows her mental state,' continued Ferran.

'So what happened in Barcelona?' Ferran struggled to swallow a piece of meat.

'Jaume wasn't happy with his marriage to another Englishwoman, called Sandy Shaw. They were both unhappy. He got back to Barcelona to find that she had several sex partners. They stayed together but opted to lead separate lives. Lydia sold up in England, packed in her job and came over to Barcelona in pursuit of Jaume. He, of course, didn't want to know. But she wouldn't let him go. She plagued him with phone calls, followed him and made his life hell. In the end he moved in with her for awhile.' Ferran helped himself to some more of the delightful potatoes covered in Roquefort sauce. He carried on with the tale.

'He couldn't take it and left. That's when it got really strange. He disappeared somehow and she obviously couldn't track him down. It appears to have been about two months where she lost track of him. But during this time she formed a dual personality.'

'What do you mean?'

'Well Doctor Xavier Val, of the University of Barcelona Department of Psychiatry, who has become very interested in this case and has spent many, many hours on it, reckons that Lydia Bart developed a form of delusional disorder schizophrenia. It, apparently, is deep rooted and may lie dormant in someone who has suffered severe emotional trauma. Doctor Val also believes that as Lydia started to use LSD heavily, almost daily, in Barcelona after Jaume rejected her, this could have triggered the underlying schizophrenia.'

'I'm getting a bit lost now,' Maria revealed. 'Explain this delusional disorder schizophrenia!'

'She became two people in her mind. It appears that she wanted to become Jaume's wife so much that she started to believe that she was. That's why she became Sandie Shaw. It was the same name as his wife. The problem was that there was already a Sandy Shaw.'

'So she killed her. She got rid of anything that ruined her image of the perfect life she was thinking she was living,' reasoned Maria.

'Exactly,' confirmed Ferran.

'Doctor Val doesn't understand it fully, and he admits that he has never come across a case quite like this, but he believes that her persona of Sandie Shaw was cool and calculating, planning her actions, but as soon as she committed a murder, or whatever, she switched back to being Lydia Bart, erasing all memory of her actions. Anything that got in the way of her perfect life with Jaume was removed.'

'So she killed Sandy Shaw, Christina Reia La Portes, and the old vagrant?'

'Yes,' confirmed Ferran. 'She even planted Jaume's wallet on the vagrant to fit in with her story.'

'So what aout the incident at the Palau Sant Jordi?' queried Maria.

'It can only have been something she made up in her mind to account for the absence from her life of Jaume. God knows what she was thinking.'

'What about the blood...the red oil in the car park that forensics found?'

'It appears that there had been some goth rock band performing some weeks earlier and their stage act involved tons of the stuff,' Ferran laughed.

'What a story,' Maria gasped.

'Yeah, one of the best yet.'

'And you thought it was a case that was going to be boring.' Ferran sat back in his seat and looked at Maria coolly.

'Are you questioning my judgement?'

She laughed, reached out across the table and held both his hands.

'Your judgment is perfect. Now let's get down to serious matters, marriage!'

About the author....

Steve Kenning

Headteacher of a large secondary school in Cornwall for the past eight years.

He has written one other novel, also set in Barcelona, 'La Hermandad del Noveno Noviembre (The Brotherhood of the Ninth of November), and a self-management, personal growth book, 'Being Annoyingly Positive.'

He lives in Devon and in Barcelona.

www.barca-only.com

pensadores futuros

Other books by Steve Kenning:

La Hermandad del Noveno Noviembre (The Brotherhood of the Ninth of November)

Published by Exposure Publishing in 2006
ISBN 1-84685-307-9

An extract from the thriller:

We looked at each other. We were scared and the tension, provided by Detective Ferran's lack of ability to protect us, filled the room. Eventually the detective spoke.
'You must realise that there is a lot of important information in this case. So far seven of the original twelve players in FC Llotja are dead, five have died in the last few days. This is a serious situation and one which is taxing the whole of the Mossos d'la Esquadra.' He looked away from us and sipped at the water. He looked dreadful.
'I must tell you that we found evidence of recent visitors to the home of Jordi Torras. We do not think that he was alone when he died.'
'You think he was murdered?'
My mind was still racing.
'You know that we did not go inside his apartment....the old lady saw us outside.'
'You are not suspects....do not worry. However, his death may not be as straightforward as it first seemed.'

Available from Amazon.co.uk
Or from: www.barca-only.com

Positivity

The Art of Personal Mastery

A Handbook to Inspire

An extract from this personal growth/self-help book:

Just imagine what would happen to the economy, to crime figures, etc if we all felt good about ourselves most of the time.

The central philosophy behind this book is to grow the individual person: individual growth. Because if we can <u>satisfy</u> the need for people......
- *to understand themselves*
- *to **recognise their strengths and weaknesses***
- *to see a <u>value to self-improvement</u>*

*.... then their **capacity** for self-development should increase along with their feeling of self-worth.*

*Central to the philosophy of individual growth is the belief that we all have an **unending potential to be better** (or to improve ourselves).*

Available from: www.barca-only.com

Printed in the United Kingdom
by Lightning Source UK Ltd.
116011UKS00001B/4-51